JANE DALY

Billionaire Next Door

Jane Daly

Copyright © 2025 by Jane Daly
Published by Forget Me Not Romances, an imprint of Winged Publications

Editor: Cynthia Hickey
Book Design by Forget Me Not Romances

All rights reserved. No part of this publication may be reproduced, stored in a retrieval system, or transmitted in any form or by any means—electronic, mechanical, photocopying, recording, or otherwise—without the prior written permission of
the publisher. The only exception is brief quotations in printed reviews. Piracy is illegal. Thank you for respecting the hard work of this author.

This book is a work of fiction. Names, characters, Places, incidents, and dialogues are either products of the author's imagination or used fictitiously.
Any resemblance to actual persons, living or dead, or events is coincidental. Scripture quotations from The Authorized (King James) Version.

Fiction and Literature: Inspirational
Christian Romance

ISBN-13:978-1-968792-08-4

Chapter 1

"I can't thank you enough for getting me this gig," Kayleigh said into her phone to her bestie, Samantha.

"You sounded desperate. I couldn't let you be homeless. Besides, the Donaldsons were desperate too. Their regular pet sitter had a last-minute family emergency."

Nerves fluttered in Kayleigh's stomach. This was almost as bad as preperformance nerves. "I hope they like me."

Samantha's laugh boomed through the phone. "What's not to like? It won't matter anyway, since they'll be out of the country, and you'll be living in a beautiful home on Seneca Lake."

The Uber driver caught her eye in the rear-view mirror. "We're here."

"Gotta go," Kayleigh said. "Talk soon."

The driver slowed to make a left turn. The tires crunched on the decomposed granite driveway. Around a curve sat a huge house curtained by white oak and hemlock trees. The driver pulled the car up to a brick porch and stopped.

"Need help with your things?"

Kayleigh took a moment to do a few yoga breaths before answering. "I'm good." She climbed out, extended the handle of her suitcase and reached into the car for her backpack and guitar case.

Kayleigh released her death-grip on the handle of her rolling suitcase and smoothed down her skirt. The massive double front doors reminded her of a Scottish castle, except for their bright red color. She pressed on the doorbell and half-expected to be greeted by a kilt-wearing butler.

"I'll be right there." The woman's voice sounded tinny through the Ring doorbell camera.

A few minutes later, the door swung open. "There you are," the woman exclaimed. "Come in out of this heat."

Kayleigh stepped into the hall and froze, mouth open. She could barely absorb the grandeur of the house.

The woman seemed impervious to Kayleigh's awe.

"I'm glad we finally get to meet in person." She put out her hand to shake Kayleigh's. "I'm Sandra. Thanks so much for being here to take care of Luna and Rocky."

Kayleigh closed her mouth and shook Sandra's hand. "Nice to meet you."

Sandra's blunt-cut bob swung around her pointed chin as she turned to head into the interior of the mansion.

"Come this way, and I'll introduce you."

Sandra led the way down the entrance hall and into a large kitchen overlooking the backyard. Two Siberian

Huskies stood at the sliding door, their breath making circles of condensation on the glass. Spying their dog mom, they jumped on the glass, shaking it.

"Get down, kids," Sandra said, cracking open the door. "Sit."

Neither dog obeyed her. Instead, they forced themselves through the small opening and sniffed Kayleigh's legs.

She bent down and scratched each of them with one hand. "Good dogs."

Sandra's voice rose an octave. "Luna and Rocky, this is Kayleigh. You behave yourselves while she's babysitting you." Her voice dropped to address Kayleigh. "I left detailed instructions on the counter. You have my cell and Robert's too, should anything arise needing our attention. I left a prepaid debit card for incidental expenses. There's three thousand dollars on it. Let me know if you need more. I've already Venmo'd half of your fee. As we discussed, I'll pay the second half when we return."

Kayleigh's head spun from the information Sandra launched in her direction. They'd talked multiple times on the phone before Sandra hired her. She'd stressed the importance of making sure the dogs got plenty of exercise and attention.

"You've come highly recommended by your friend, Samantha, and her husband, Logan."

"Thank you." Kayleigh silently thanked her for the generous amount of money she'd be paid for this four-week dog-sitting gig.

"The housekeeper comes every Friday. She'll clean and do laundry, but she doesn't cook. Use the debit card to buy food." Sandra's eyes pinned Kayleigh. "But no parties. Understood?"

"Yes, ma'am." The 'ma'am' came out naturally after living in Nashville for six months. "No parties."

A man Kayleigh assumed to be Sandra's husband entered the kitchen.

"Our ride is here, sweetie." He strode to Kayleigh and extended his hand. "You must be Kayleigh. I'm Robert. Very nice to meet you."

His six-foot-plus height dwarfed Sandra by at least six inches.

"Thank you. I hope you have a nice trip."

Sandra beamed. "We haven't been to Europe since our youngest graduated from high school. I can't wait." She cast a longing glance at Robert. "I couldn't convince Robert to take more than four weeks off."

Robert smiled down at his petite wife. "You'll be desperate to come home by then."

Sandra leaned over and planted a kiss on each dog's head. "Be good, children."

Kayleigh resisted the urge to roll her eyes. Like the Kendrick Lamar song, the uber wealthy were "Not Like Us."

Sandra glanced around the kitchen as if trying to make sure she'd covered every eventuality. "I left detailed instructions on the counter."

"Come on, sweetie. Let's not keep the driver waiting."

Sandra and Robert swept out of the kitchen in a cloud of scent. Sandra turned when they reached the front door and waved. "Bye bye, darlings." She blew a kiss in the direction of the dogs.

Once the front door clicked shut, Kayleigh breathed a sigh of relief. "Well, doggies, it's just you and me now."

She circled the concrete-topped island and found the instructions Sandra left. It was several pages long and spiral bound.

"I love your mom," Kayleigh said to the pups who lounged at her feet. Sandra was detailed to a fault with all the information she'd need to housesit and dog sit.

Feeding schedule: Twice a day at 7:00 a.m. and 5:00 p.m. Food is in the refrigerator and should be warmed 30 seconds before serving. Food shipments arrive every Monday. Treats can be given sparingly.

Sandra included vet phone numbers—daytime and nighttime. Emergency contact information, doctors, yard service—she'd left nothing to chance.

"I've never met anyone as organized as I am," Kayleigh said. One of the dogs, Luna maybe, slapped her tail on the travertine floor.

Kayleigh returned to the entrance hall and retrieved her suitcase and backpack. She'd come back down for her guitar. She lugged her stuff up the curved staircase and stopped at the end of a long hallway. Which bedroom would she be staying in?

She returned downstairs and thumbed through Sandra's instruction manual. Sure enough, Sandra had included a floor plan with Kayleigh's guest room circled. Kayleigh shook her head with a smile. Sandra wasn't as organized as Kayleigh. Sandra was miles above her.

Kayleigh couldn't resist opening every cupboard to admire the extent of Sandra's organization. Sure enough, every cupboard was neatly labeled.

"Wow." This lady must have a PhD in organizational management. But when Kayleigh opened the pantry door, her mouth dropped open.

Every shelf was neatly arranged by type of food, size of packaging, and labeled with what went where.

"Holy cats. I am officially in awe." Sandra must have a bit of obsessive-compulsive disorder. Kayleigh was reminded of her own habit of creating organization out of chaos.

Her stomach growled. "Time for lunch," she said to the dogs. She tossed them a treat and fixed a salad while they chomped on their treats.

Kayleigh opened the back door and let Luna and Rocky out. They bounded across the deck, down the steps and galloped to the bushes at the end of the manicured lawn.

Kayleigh sat on the deck steps and watched them sniff, pee, and sniff some more. This should be an easy gig. Four weeks of living in luxury would give her tons of time to work on her next few songs.

She stood, brushed down her skirt and went into the house to retrieve her guitar. She returned in time to see Luna and Rocky disappear into the bushes on one side of the yard. Then she heard barking and a man yelling.

What in the Sam Hill?

Holden finished his last of ten laps in his swimming pool and pulled himself onto the steps, using the handrail he'd had installed.

"Swimming will be the best way to regain strength," his physical therapist had said.

Holden's lungs ached, and he shook with fatigue. Cancer sucked.

As he hauled himself to the pool deck, two mutts

burst through the thick bushes separating his property from the one next door. They sprang over the low brick wall and charged toward him, barking.

"No! Down!" The mutts paid him no mind.

No more than a minute later, a woman appeared in the gap, ducking to avoid hitting her head on low-hanging branches. Her red hair glowed like a beacon in the late afternoon sun. Holden took in her sleeveless top, denim skirt that brushed the top of her knees, and scuffed cowboy boots.

Her face was a mask of alarm. "I'm so sorry. Luna. Rocky. No. Down." She tried unsuccessfully to grab the dog's collars.

"How did they get in here?" Holden demanded. He steadied himself with the handrail, scowling at his cane that lay against one of the patio chairs. With the furballs between him and it, he'd have to stand there half-naked and dripping until he could reach it without stumbling.

"I think they dug a hole under the fence. And broke it too." The woman looked ready to cry.

"Good grief. I don't need this." Holden sucked in a breath and blew it out. "Hand me a towel." He held out a hand and waited for the woman to pluck a swim towel off the patio table and thrust it in his direction.

"I-I'll get it fixed," she said, avoiding looking at him.

"See that you do." Holden used his free hand to rub the towel over his head and down his chest. "Who are you and why are you in the Donaldson's back yard?"

Her face flamed almost as red as her hair. "I'm housesitting. If you're so familiar with your neighbors, you'd know they're in Europe for four weeks." Her voice shook with outrage.

Holden took a moment to process her words. On a few occasions, he and Robert Donaldson had exchanged friendly waves and a few words. He didn't recall Robert mentioning anything about being gone. How would he and Sandra feel if they knew their house sitter had let their spoiled Huskies dig through the yard?

The woman placed her hands on her hips in a defiant gesture. Her chin rose an inch or two. "I said I'm sorry. I'll get someone out here to fix the fence."

"And fill in the hole."

"And fill in the hole," she repeated.

Holden held back a smile at her feistiness. He was still annoyed that he'd been caught in a weak moment. He needed for her to go back to the Donaldson's so he could retrieve his cane and return to the sanctity of his home.

An uncomfortable silence grew as he took in her measure. Most people felt compelled to fill in a silence. This woman did not. She merely glared at him with eyes like ice picks.

"Well, then. I suggest you take the dogs back home."

"I will." She looked ready to say something else but must have decided against it.

She grabbed the mutt's collars and hauled them toward the planter. "Again, I apologize." Her back was stiff as she stepped over the low brick wall.

"Sorry doesn't fix the problem." Holden wanted to grab the words back the moment they'd escaped.

She whipped around to face him, her eyes ablaze. "Are y'all always this grumpy?"

"Yes."

She held his gaze for a moment before ducking

under the low-hanging bushes. Holden watched her backside until she'd disappeared into the hedge. He should have gotten her name.

He limped to the table and pulled out a chair. The woman's question stabbed his conscience. Since his diagnosis and subsequent treatment, he had been grumpy, grouchy, and out of sorts. But to take out his ire against a lowly house sitter was unconscionable.

Holden's mother's voice echoed in his brain. "A soft answer turns away wrath, but a harsh word stirs up anger."

Yes, Mom. I know. I'm a jerk.

JANE DALY

Chapter 2

Kayleigh dragged Luna and Rocky toward the house, promising them a treat if they did as she said.

"The nerve of that guy. Some people think they can talk down to others. His mama shoulda taught him better." Kayleigh's words had no impact on the recalcitrant dogs. They swarmed around her legs, impatient for their reward.

She was still fuming when her phone range ten minutes later.

"Hi, Mom."

"Kayleigh, you were supposed to call me when you arrived."

"I'm sorry." How many times would she have to apologize before the day was over? "I'm here in one piece."

"Are you sure you'll be okay by yourself for a month? I can come stay for a week or so."

Kayleigh made a face before responding. "That's sweet, Mom, but I'll be fine." Mom was less a helicopter parent and more a drone, swooping in to try and save Kayleigh from herself. Maybe she should have stayed in Nashville, miles away from New York both physically and culturally. Except for the pesky problem of not having a place to live.

"You'll let me know if you change your mind?"

Time to steer Mom in another direction. "Of course. How was Aunt Marnie's birthday party?"

"So much fun," Mom gushed. "She planned a scavenger hunt in New York City. "

"How did that work?"

"Oh, you know your aunt. She is Miss Party Planner. She gave us all a list of things we had to do while in the City. Take a selfie in front of the charging bull statue in the Financial District, buy a lottery ticket at a bodega, take a photo of a street performer. Stuff like that."

"Sounds fun. How did Granny do?"

"She kept up with your dad and me. I'm amazed that someone her age is still so spry."

"Tell Granny I'll call her soon. Love to you and Dad."

Kayleigh disconnected and retrieved the spiral bound tome Sandra had left. She thumbed through the pages, searching for any clues for what to do in the case of a broken fence.

Which brought her back to annoyance at the next-door neighbor. She'd tried not to gape at his chest as he stood at the edge of his swimming pool, water dripping down his thin torso. Blue eyes, short, dark hair cut military short. Yeah, he was smokin' hot. But not a nice person. Kayleigh's strict Christian upbringing didn't allow her to call him a derogatory name. Unfortunately.

Hand me a towel. Fix the fence. Used to ordering people around and having others do his bidding.

She found the name, phone number, and email of the landscape maintenance company in Sandra's binder.

Kayleigh sent an email identifying herself as the Donaldson's house sitter and asking if fence repair was part of his contract.

Satisfied she'd done all she could, she retrieved her guitar from where she'd left it at the foot of the stairs and carried it outside. Luna and Rocky eyed her from their comfy beds on the kitchen floor.

"I'm going outside, guys." Rocky did a combination yawn/yelp in reply.

The Donaldson's yard sloped down to a low gate between two brick pillars. Sandra had told her there was a path leading to Seneca Lake. Tomorrow, she'd leash the dogs and explore.

The quiet of early evening was broken only by the call of geese soaring over the water before nesting for the night. Kayleigh sat on the top step of the wood deck and strummed the strings to warm up.

Kayleigh had four weeks to finish six songs for a demo tape. The music producer she'd connected with in Nashville said she needed a minimum of six original songs. She'd paid him a deposit to hold her spot for the recording studio. It had taken all her savings. But the pressure to produce more songs had created writer's block.

She had a month here in this gorgeous mansion on Seneca Lake to get her mojo back.

Her fingers stroked the guitar. She began to sing her go-to warmup song, *Killing Me Softly*. The vocal range perfectly matched hers. Soon, she was lost in the words and the melody, leaving all the stress and angst of the day behind.

Until the vision of the cranky next-door neighbor invaded her Zen. Something in his eyes spoke of deep hurt. Instead of hating on him for barking orders in her direction, Kayleigh imagined what hurt he'd experienced.

Right. As if billionaires had problems like normal people.

Holden frowned and flung his phone at one of the decorative pillows on his king-sized bed.

"Why now?" His words echoed from the ten-foot ceiling. His assistant wasn't supposed to start maternity leave for another month.

"I have preeclampsia," Donna had said. "The doctor wants me on complete bedrest until the baby comes."

"What am I supposed to do?" Holden had demanded.

Donna's words did nothing to calm his ire. "You'll figure it out, H. You always do."

Holden grabbed his cane and strode to the windows overlooking the deck. He stepped out and limped to the railing, staring down at the aqua light of the pool. The water sat smooth and placid, unlike his mood.

How was he supposed to operate his company and avoid the board of directors without Donna to run interference? The nine-person board was making noises about when he would return to work. Since the debacle with his former friend and business partner, and Holden's cancer treatment, they were right to be worried.

In the distance, Holden saw the pinpricks of light dotting the lake's coastline. The sound of guitar music drew him to the left side of the deck. Someone was singing. Not someone. The red-haired beauty from next door.

Killing Me Softly. The words floated up to him in the soft evening breeze. How apropos for his life at that moment. The cancer had been killing him softly before it was diagnosed.

"We expect complete remission," his oncologist had said.

Yeah, after nearly killing him with the treatment. They'd said he'd be back to his former physical health in less than six months. But what about his emotional health? His best friend and business partner's betrayal still felt like a wooden stake in his heart.

The woman next door stopped playing. Holden leaned over the railing to see if she was still there. She'd put her guitar back in its case and sat with her arms hugged around her knees. He should have asked her name.

As if feeling his stare, the woman glanced over and up to his deck. Holden shrank back into the shadows. He sank onto a deck chair, hoping she'd continue singing. Her voice reminded him of a distant memory, of his mother singing him to sleep after one of his many nightmares.

The ping of her phone carried the sound on the soft evening breeze. Holden heard her answer and leaned forward to listen.

"Yes, I'm here. The house is amazing. The next four weeks will be epic."

The person on the other end must have been talking. He cringed when the woman spoke again.

"You'll never believe what happened. And on my first day, too. The dogs somehow broke through the fence connecting the house next door."

A pause. Holden held his breath waiting for what might come next.

"The guy who lives there was super ticked. Talk about Mr. Grumpy Pants."

Holden cringed. 'Mr. Grumpy Pants.' He'd been called a lot of names, but that wasn't one. Brilliant negotiator, ruthless businessman, cold-hearted, yes. Grumpy Pants, no.

She continued. "Too bad he's smoking hot. Otherwise, we could have been friends."

Holden smiled to himself. She thought he was hot.

"Well, I better go. I have to check on the pups once more and hit the sack. Love you, too."

She had a boyfriend. Figured. Women as gorgeous as her didn't stay single for long. A chill spread over his arms as the temperature dropped. The wind shifted, bringing cold, wet air from the lake.

Before his illness, he'd been impervious to the elements. Now the slightest dip in the temp had him reaching for a sweatshirt.

Inside, Holden glanced at the bed and decided he wasn't tired enough for sleep. He headed into his office and sank into the ergonomic leather chair behind the cherry wood desk. Pulling his laptop close, he checked the email for an update from his attorney. Nothing.

How long did it take to get a court date after filing charges for embezzlement? David was out on bail, pending a court date. The unfairness of it irritated Holden to the nth degree. Why should David be allowed to go free while Holden had to deal with the fallout from his thievery.

Holden had treated David like a brother. They'd often joked that their relationship was akin to King

David and Jonathan. Holden snorted. More like Cain and Abel, except for the killing part. Instead, David had planted a knife in Holden's back and twisted it.

Holden vowed to never let anyone take advantage of him again.

So why did his thoughts turn to the gorgeous woman next door? Would she try to blame him for the broken fence? Sure, he had the means to pay for it. But the Donaldson's mutts had broken the fence. If the slats had rotted, it was as much his neighbor's fault as his.

Holden frowned, remembering how she'd avoided looking at him when she thrust the towel into his hands. He hadn't gained back much of the weight he'd lost during chemo and radiation. His bathroom mirror reflected the loss of muscle in his arms and legs.

Still, she'd told her boyfriend he was 'smokin' hot.'

Holden filed that bit of information into a mental safe and locked the door.

JANE DALY

Chapter 3

Kayleigh woke with a start to find two wet noses planted on her out-flung arm. "Good morning, mutts." She swung her legs over the side of the bed with a yawn.

"Bet you two want to go out." As if understanding her words, they padded to the bedroom door. "Let me take care of my business, and then, I'll let you take care of your business."

Downstairs, Kayleigh slid the door open. "Stay away from Mr. Grumpy Pants," she called as Luna and Rocky bounded toward the far end of the property.

While the dogs sniffed the bushes for any new scents, Kayleigh retrieved their food from the fridge. Sandra had left precise instructions on how to heat their meals and which bowls to use. By the time she'd finished, Luna and Rocky had planted their noses on the door, their tongues hanging out.

She let them in, and they headed straight for their breakfast. While they scarfed down their food, Kayleigh used Sandra's information on how to operate the espresso machine. After two failed attempts, the kitchen filled with the satisfying scent of hot java.

Kayleigh carried her mug to the back deck and

inhaled. The smell of coffee mixed nicely with the humid air. "It's going to be a hot one," she said aloud. Maybe she'd put on her swimsuit and walk down to Seneca Lake today. The dogs would enjoy the walk, too.

She strolled to the hedge where Rocky and Luna and broken the fence. She stepped into the trampled bushes to peer at the ragged edges of wood.

She jerked upright and smacked her head on a low branch when a male voice spoke.

"What are you doing?"

Kayleigh rubbed the growing bump on her head. "What does it look like I'm doing?"

Instead of answering her question, the grumpy guy from next door said, "I've made arrangements for the fence to be repaired tomorrow."

Kayleigh peered through the foliage. Why did someone so insanely gorgeous have to act like he was snake bit?

"How'd you get someone to respond so quickly?" Kayleigh hadn't expected to hear from Sandra's landscape guy until at least the afternoon.

"I have people."

Of course he did. Rich people had people. Poor people, like her, had . . . well, she had a personality. Unlike the Adonis-like creature frowning at her through the thicket.

"Come over here."

Kayleigh bit her lip to keep from asking for a 'pretty please.' She stepped over the broken fence slats and onto his side of the hedge.

"What do you want?" she asked, answering his frown with her own.

"I have to be gone tomorrow when the fence repair guy is here. I'll write a check, and you can give it to them when they're done."

"Don't you have people for that too?"

It seemed impossible for the guy's frown to deepen, but it did. "Not tomorrow. My housekeeper has the day off, and my assistant is on maternity leave."

Kayleigh eyed him, taking in how heavily he seemed to lean on his cane. Maybe he was in pain and that caused him to be a such a mess. He turned around and limped across the pool deck toward the back door of his house.

"Hurry up," he said when he reached the sliding glass door.

Kayleigh caught up to him and followed as he led the way into his house. The open floor plan felt spacious except for the massive amount of wood covering the walls and ceiling. She supposed the look was to make one feel like they were part of the forest surrounding the area. But the walls seemed to press in.

"Come with me," he said, heading across the room to a staircase.

Kayleigh felt a flash of alarm. "I'll wait here." What if this guy was a predator? Alone, in this mansion, no one would hear her if she screamed for help.

"Good grief, woman, I'm not here to entice you into some illicit behavior. My office is upstairs, as is my checkbook."

Kayleigh returned his gaze without flinching.

He broke the silence. "My housekeeper is upstairs if that makes you feel better."

"Only slightly."

The guy turned and closed the distance between

them. "I'm Holden Jeffries," he said, moving his cane from his right hand to left. He extended his hand to shake hers. If it was possible, the man was even better looking fully clothed than in his swim trunks. Tan slacks and a teal golf shirt that hung loosely on his slim frame. Brown loafers. Close-cropped hair and a shadow of a beard. Her gaze focused on the cleft in the middle of his chin.

Kayleigh let him clasp her hand, surprised at its warmth. "Kayleigh McGuire." He held her hand longer than longer than was the social norm. Kayleigh felt like she'd swallowed a bird in flight. Why did this grump affect her like this?

Blue eyes bored into hers. "Now that introductions are out of the way, come upstairs so I can write a check."

"Why don't I wait down here?" *So I can catch my breath.*

A flash of pain spread across Holden's face. "I don't want to have to come downstairs again." He lifted the cane and set it down with a decisive *thunk.* "In case you haven't noticed, mobility isn't my best feature."

Kayleigh felt a stab of sympathy. It disappeared when he spoke again.

"You going to stand there all day, or are you coming up?"

Sheesh. The guy was insufferable.

"Fine," she said, but his back was already turned as he took the stairs one at a time.

What had happened to make him so ornery? Her mind spun with possibilities as she crafted a country song, describing a rodeo accident and a broken cowboy.

Something about breaking his back didn't hurt as

much as the pain inflicted on his heart.

This next four weeks would be just the thing to get her song-writing juices flowing.

Holden's breath caught when he clasped Kayleigh's hand. The tips of her fingers were calloused, most likely from playing guitar. It had been a long time since he'd felt the touch of a woman's hand. His physical therapist, oncologist, and massage therapist were all male. He didn't expect a jolt of pleasure at his brief contact with her.

Pain in his leg radiated up his spine as he navigated the stairs. He clenched his jaw against white-hot jabs and concentrated on not stumbling. No way would he let himself look weak in front of the red-headed beauty behind him.

At the top of the stairs, he turned. Kayleigh had paused to look down on the living room.

"Follow me," Holden said, limping down the wide hall to the open space he used as his office. He walked around the desk and shuffled the papers and files sitting on top, searching for his business checkbook.

He glanced up to see Kayleigh frown. "What?"

"Your office. It's a mess."

"My assistant went on maternity leave." If Donna had been here, she'd have taken care of the fence repair. She would have figured out how to pay electronically, saving him the time and energy to write a check. His desk would be tidy the way he liked it. Donna would have sorted the mail, checked his calendar, and taken care of the trivial details that drove him nuts.

"Can I help?"

Holden glared at her. "No. Stay here while I see if I took the checkbook into my bedroom."

He made his way down the hall to the master bedroom, his knuckles white on the cane. First stop was the bathroom to dry swallow a pain pill. He'd promised himself to back down on them, but today's pain level demanded relief.

The edge of the king-sized bed gave as Holden sank down, hoping for quick reprieve from the ever-present ache. He lay back, huffing a few breaths out as the pressure on his hip joint eased.

Doctors said they'd caught the cancer before it spread into his lymph nodes. But the lingering weakness infuriated him. The latest report had Holden reeling.

"You might consider a hip replacement," Dr. Ahmed suggested. "But not until you regain your strength."

"And when will that be," Holden had demanded.

"That's up to you. Eat healthy, do your exercises, and avoid stress."

Holden huffed out a humorless laugh. Avoiding stress was like avoiding breathing. His board of directors wanted to know how Holden planned to recoup the money David had stolen.

He had no idea. Conversations with Dad didn't help either. David had been extradited back into the United States, but the money trail had gone cold. It was either invested in the Cayman's or spent on some luxurious lifestyle stuff.

Holden pushed himself to a sitting position and used his cane to help him stand. He returned to his home office to find the redhead sitting behind his desk.

Kayleigh jerked upright when Holden spoke. "What have you done?" he demanded.

"I-I'm sorry?" Kayleigh cringed at the way her voice rose. She couldn't help herself. The messy desk pulled her like a deer to a salt lick.

She shot to her feet and shoved the leather desk chair back with her thighs. It hit the wall with a thunk. "I found your checkbook." She pointed to the book now lying front and center on the massive desk.

"You touched my things." Holden strode around the desk, the cane punching the floor.

"I straightened your desk," Kayleigh said. "No need to get your pants in a wad." Her Irish temper flared. "I thought you'd be grateful." Perhaps the word wasn't in this guy's vocabulary.

Holden's mouth had formed a grim line. "You invaded my privacy."

How could she explain her compulsive need to organize? "But I found your checkbook."

Holden's posture seemed to relax. He sank onto the desk chair. Kayleigh had no choice but to move out of the way.

"Yes, you did. Let me write a check."

Kayleigh stared at the top of Holden's head as he bent over the checkbook. His dark hair looked buzz-cut. Her mind wandered to his use of the cane. Maybe he'd been injured in combat.

A new song formed in her brain.
When I left you I was a whole man
Now I'm half a man and you're gone
Kayleigh chewed on her bottom lip. Not a great

start, but she'd work on the lyrics later. She glanced up to find Holden watching her with narrowed eyes.

"What?" she asked.

"Sit down for a minute. I have a proposition for you."

Sweat formed on the back of Kayleigh's neck. A proposition? That sounded ominous. She sat on the edge of one of the chairs facing his desk, ready to jump up if this went sideways. She'd easily outrun him to the stairs.

"I need an assistant, and you seem capable."

Capable? Was that supposed to be a compliment? Kayleigh waited in silence for him to continue.

"I'm offering you a job. Short-term."

"I have a job." The Donaldsons wouldn't be back for a month, and there was no way she'd give up the money they'd offered. She'd have enough to pay first and last month rent on an apartment in Nashville, plus a little extra to tide her over until she found a job.

"I am well aware of that. You can do both."

Kayleigh shook her head. "I don't think so." She had enough on her plate with caring for Luna and Rocky and working on more songs.

"I'll pay you double whatever the Donaldsons are paying you."

Double? Who had that kind of money?

"You're kidding," Kayleigh said.

"I can assure you I am not. Kidding."

Yeah, he probably had no humor hiding in that gorgeous head. It was a shame, really, that someone so handsome was without a discernible personality.

Holden rose to his feet. "You can start tomorrow."

As if she'd already falling in with his plans.

"I'll need to think about it." Kayleigh stood and faced him across the desk.

"What is there to think about?" Holden's face was back to its customary frown.

Kayleigh ran through several responses, but none that she wanted to say out loud. Granny's voice echoed in her ears. "If you can't say anything nice, don't say anything at all."

"Look, Mr. Jeffries, as wonderful as it sounds to work with you," Kayleigh couldn't keep the sarcasm from her voice. "I need time to think about your offer."

"How much time?"

Kayleigh sighed. "I will get back to you tomorrow. Will that work for your timetable?"

"Fine." Holden reached for one of the business cards in a holder on the front of his desk. "Here's my card. My cell number is on it. I'll expect your call tomorrow before five pm."

Kayleigh shook her head. This guy was unbelievable. No wonder his assistant quit. No, not quit. She was on maternity leave. Good for her. Dealing with a newborn would be easier than working with this dictator.

Kayleigh took the card and the check he'd written and tucked them into her shorts pocket. She turned and left his office and clomped down the stairs without another word.

JANE DALY

Chapter 4

Kayleigh jogged across Holden's stamped concrete patio and dashed through the opening in the fence. The dogs still lay on their beds in the corner of the kitchen. They thumped their tails twice before closing their eyes again.

She stared unfocused at their prone bodies. What just happened? She'd gone from her roommate kicking her out of their apartment in Nashville, to a cushy dog-sitting job, to another job offer from a guy who could pose as a model in GQ.

Which brought her thoughts around to her best friend and former model, Samantha. Kayleigh pulled out her phone and dialed Sam's number.

"Hey, girl, I was just thinking about you." Sam's voice warmed Kayleigh and immediately calmed her.

"I hope all good thoughts."

"Of course. I wanted to check in and see how it's going with the world's most spoiled dogs."

Kayleigh strolled into the Donaldson's living room and sank onto a bronze leather sofa. "The dogs are no problem. Well, except they dug under the fence to the house next door and managed to destroy the fence."

"Oh, no! Did you get it fixed? I'm pretty sure the

Donaldsons have a yard maintenance guy."

Kayleigh put the phone on speaker so she could do a quick check of her email. "He says he can't be here until next week."

"Did the pups get into the next-door neighbor's backyard?"

"Oh, yeah." Kayleigh told Sam about her initial meeting with Holden Jeffries.

Sam laughed. "I met him once when Logan and I were at a fundraiser. It's been a couple years, though. Is he still drop-dead gorgeous?"

Kayleigh took a moment to answer. Good looks did not overshadow the fact that he was a jerk. *Sorry, Granny, but it's true.*

"He is extremely handsome, but not a nice person."

"You might Google him, Kay. I seem to remember something about a health scare."

"I will. But wait until you hear this. He wants me to do admin work for him."

"And this is a bad thing? You get to work with a hunk of a man who is easy on the eyes and make some side money."

"I was hoping you'd tell me it was a bad idea."

"Will it interfere with dog-sitting?"

"No."

"Then, what's the problem?"

Kayleigh took a moment to respond. The problem was that Holden was uber handsome, and Kayleigh couldn't help being attracted to him. Working for him and with him might prove too much of a distraction.

But the money …

"I'm waiting," Sam said.

"Fine. I'll do it. And if I hate it, I'm blaming you."

Sam laughed. "I can take it. But you must promise to keep me posted. Who knows, you might find true love in Mr. Holden Jeffries. Just like I did. Right next door."

Kayleigh smiled despite herself. "Like that's gonna happen."

"You never know, girlfriend."

Kayleigh set the check and Holden's business card on the cherry-wood coffee table, smoothing out the fold and the wrinkles from being in her pocket. 'Holden Holdings' read the name on the account. Same on the business card. He'd made the check out to Finger Lakes Construction Services for the whopping sum of five thousand dollars. How in the Sam Hill did a simple fence repair cost that much?

Girl, you aren't in Nashville anymore.

Holden checked his phone for the location of his driver. He was about ten minutes away.

"Tara, I'm going into the City for a meeting. I'll be back tomorrow.

His housekeeper, Tara, was wiping down the marble kitchen countertops. "Okay, Mr. H. I am off tomorrow, remember?"

"I remember." He'd forgotten. Donna had always taken care of details like that.

He limped to the front door and stood on the front porch to wait for his car. He carried a satchel containing his laptop and a few files he needed to peruse on the drive from Seneca Lake to New York City. If Donna was here, she'd have briefed him on the important details he'd need for his board meeting. He ground his teeth in frustration.

Would his lovely neighbor, Kayleigh, accept his offer? It might take a few days to get her up to speed, but it would be worth the effort so he could concentrate on getting his strength back. Plus, he'd get to know her better.

He'd been intrigued the minute she'd stepped through the hedge bordering his and the Donaldson's yard. Blazing red hair and a personality to match. Holden didn't know any women who wore cowboy boots. The women he'd dated, precancer, wore impossibly high heels and designer clothing. Since his diagnosis and treatment, he'd avoided the opposite sex. No woman wanted a man who was damaged.

Even his board was having second thoughts about his ability to lead. He mentally cursed his former friend, David. And immediately repented. The Bible talked about forgiving your enemies, up to seventy times. In one day.

Holden shook his head. Seemed impossible. David had taken Holden's money, and worse, he'd taken advantage of Holden's trust.

A dark SUV pulled into Holden's driveway. Holden got to his feet, retrieved his satchel, and walked down the brick steps to meet the car.

His driver hopped out and hurried around to the back passenger door. "Morning, Mr. Jeffries."

"I think it's afternoon, Henry." Holden climbed in, fastened his seatbelt, and pulled the stack of files from his satchel.

By the time they reached the City, Holden was prepared for the board meeting.

"I'll call the meeting to order," Holden said, taking his seat at the head of the twelve-person table. "Thank you all for coming. We have a lot on the agenda today. I apologize for not sending the agenda ahead of time. You may have heard Donna has taken a leave of absence."

A few murmurs of assent echoed in the cavernous conference room.

One of the board members raised her hand. "Holden, have you made arrangements for her replacement? I can have my assistant put out some feelers for a temp."

"That won't be necessary. I made an offer to someone today. She promised to get back with me tomorrow." Holden hoped Kayleigh would agree. If she didn't, he didn't know what he would do.

One of the older board members spoke up. "We need to talk finances. Our balance sheet has taken a hit. What is your plan?"

Holden stared at him until the other man dropped his gaze. This particular board member, Stanley Morehouse, wanted the CEO position. Holden had a suspicion Stanley was working behind his back to get a vote of 'no confidence.' Stanley never would've dared if Holden's dad were still CEO.

Holden opted not to address Stanley's question directly. "If you will turn your attention to page three of the report in front of you, you'll see there's a proposal for the purchase of our property in Texas. If we sell it, the funds will go a long way toward recouping our loss."

Stanley poked a finger at the proposal. "But we'll lose the monthly revenue from that property. How is that a win?"

Holden spoke through clenched jaws. "Turn the page, Morehouse."

He caught am amused glance from one of the female members. He could count on Marjorie to be on his side. She'd worked with his dad since the day he took over from Holden's grandpa.

"I'd like to make a motion," Marjorie said. "I move we sell the Texas property."

"Second," echoed one of the others.

Holden glanced at the secretary to be sure she'd recorded the motion and second.

"Wait just a gol durn minute," Stanley said. "We need to discuss this."

"According to Robert's Rules of Order, we have a motion and a second, and we can now entertain discussion." Holden dared Morehouse to argue.

There ensued a lively discussion about the pros and cons of the sale, but the motion passed. Holden's hip ached like crazy, and he hoped the meeting would be concluded before he lost his temper.

Stanley Morehouse spoke up after the vote. "Before anyone makes a motion to close the meeting, we need to talk about the ongoing leadership of this company."

A hot flush worked its way up from Holden's neck. How dare he! Moorehouse would never have made such a move if Holden's dad was still here.

"Speak your mind, Morehouse. We're all dying to hear what you have to say."

Most of the board kept their eyes focused on the papers in front of them. One other man who always sided with Stanley swept his gaze from Holden to Moorehouse.

Stanley inhaled and blew out the breath. "I think I speak for all of us here that we're concerned about your extended absence from the company."

Marjorie looked ready to explode. "The man had cancer, Stan. Show some compassion."

Stanley raised his hands in surrender. "It's obvious the company has suffered without someone at the helm. I just think we should appoint an interim CEO from the board and give Holden the opportunity to get well."

Holden sucked in a breath. 'An interim CEO.' Morehouse would, of course, accept the nomination. Before Holden could respond, Marjorie interjected.

"I move we adjourn the meeting."

"Second."

"Secretary, call for the vote," Holden said. Morehouse and his crony had no choice but to agree.

Holden stood and leaned heavily on his cane. "I will be in my apartment for the rest of today and part of tomorrow." He glanced from person to person. "If anyone would like to discuss things, feel free to call my personal cell."

Holden stomped out of the room and fled to his office. He rested his head in his hands. These were the kind of days when he wished he had someone to vent with. His dad had Mom as his sounding board. Holden used to have David, but that relationship had gone up in smoke.

His thoughts turned to Kayleigh. Then, he put her out of his mind just as quickly as it had entered. No woman wanted a man who couldn't have kids.

JANE DALY

Chapter 5

Kayleigh spent the rest of the day working on her newest song. She made a few tweaks to the lyrics and slowed the tempo.

"Perfect," she said to Luna and Rocky. They lolled at her feet, enjoying the afternoon sun. A few clouds scuttled across the sky alternating sunlight with shade.

"Tomorrow, we'll walk to the lake," she promised. She carried her guitar into the house and called the dogs in. They slurped water like they'd been in a desert for days. Kayleigh felt the same. The humidity sucked the moisture from her mouth.

She used the water dispenser on the subzero fridge to fill a tumbler and sat at the kitchen table with her laptop.

She typed 'Holden Jeffries' into the Google search bar. A photo of an elderly man appeared, along with an article. That wasn't her hot next-door neighbor.

Continuing to scroll, she found a photo of a sixty-something man who looked a lot like Holden.

'Holden Jeffries II Fends off Hostile Takeover.' Kayleigh read through the article, noting the date. Three years ago.

Further down the page was a picture of her next-door neighbor, though his face was fuller, and he sported an impressive head of dark hair.

'Holden Jeffries III Takes The Reins.' Kayleigh shook her head. So, her handsome neighbor was third in line of a real estate dynasty. Figured.

She scrolled back up the page and typed in Holden Jeffries III. The page populated with a dozen articles, extolling Holden's real estate savvy.

'The Golden Boy Delivers Again.' Ugh. The article should have read, The Golden Boy is a Cranky Pants. Holden was pictured with a parade of stunning women, all beautiful, all skinny, and probably all plastic.

Her phone buzzed. Mom again. Kayleigh closed her laptop with a snap.

"Hi, Mom. What's up?"

"I'm glad I caught you. Granny was asking about you. She gave me an envelope to give to you. Want me to open it?"

No way. Mom was even nosier that Kayleigh was, which was saying a lot. Kayleigh's need to peer into other's cabinets and drawers had become a joke in their family.

"That's okay, Mom. Why don't you send it to me. I'll give you the Donaldson's address."

"Well, if you're sure."

Kayleigh pictured Mom slapping the envelope against her thigh, then holding it up to a light to determine its contents.

"I'm sure." Kayleigh read the address from Sandra's well-prepared instructions.

"Is everything okay?" Mom asked.

"Everything's fine, Mom. Nothing has changed since I talked to you yesterday." Nothing except that her smoking hot neighbor offered her a part-time job. Which she still hadn't responded to.

"I'm concerned about your grandma. She's been forgetful lately. And a bit clumsy. She took a tumble at the store and ended up with a bruised cheekbone."

Kayleigh's heart sped up. "Did you have her checked out at the doctor?" She and Granny had a special bond. She hated the thought of her beloved Granny getting old.

"The doctor said to keep an eye on her. Your dad and I are taking her for some tests next week."

"Good. Keep me posted."

Kayleigh disconnected and sat with her hands in her lap. Luna padded in from the kitchen and nudged Kayleigh's leg with her nose.

"It's okay, girl. I'm a little worried is all." Luna nudged Kayleigh's hand, begging for a head scratch. "Remind me to call Granny later," she said to the pup.

But first, finish exploring the house. She strode to the front door, her cowboy boots thudding on the travertine floor. She turned and surveyed the doors leading from the massive entry. To the left was the living room. Leather couches faced each other and sat perpendicular to a stone fireplace. Bookshelves lined two walls with a rolling ladder for access to the top shelf. She bypassed the curving staircase on the right and headed down the hall beyond the stairs and past the kitchen.

A few paintings hung on the wall leading down to a laundry room, bathroom, and a closed door. Kayleigh swung open the door and gasped. Sandra had a full workout room equipped with high-end equipment. Mirrors covered one wall, and another looked out onto the back yard. The floor was covered with spongy mats to absorb impact.

Kayleigh wandered around the spin bike, elliptical, and treadmill, to a rack of colorful hand weights. A big screen television hung on one wall in front of an open space. Kayleigh assumed Sandra worked out with either yoga or Pilates. No wonder she looked so good at her age.

The dogs followed Kayleigh up the stairs as she opened each door to peek into the upstairs bedrooms. She bit her lip at the door to the Donaldson's master bedroom, sticking her head in and quickly closing it. There was curious and there was intrusive. If the Donaldson's had doggie cams, Kayleigh didn't want to be caught somewhere she shouldn't be.

The three other guest rooms were just as nicely decorated as the one Sandra had chosen. Except hers had a private bathroom, which was bigger than her apartment back in Nashville. The turquoise tile bathroom floor was heated. Not that she needed heat during the summer. The two sinks along one side were glass bowls that sat on the counter and had lights around the edges. They made a great nightlight for middle-of-the-night bathroom needs.

The gigantic spa tub looked big enough to hold four people. She'd definitely be taking advantage of that during her stay. Luna and Rocky sniffed her towel, the clothes she'd dropped on the floor, and her makeup bag.

"C'mon, guys, let's go back downstairs and outside."

They galloped down the stairs ahead of her and stood at attention at the back door. Kayleigh stepped out onto the deck and shaded her eyes with her hands. The trampled down bushes where the dogs had dug reminded her that she needed to let Holden know she'd accept his offer on a temporary basis.

But might as well let him stew overnight.

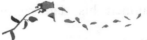

Holden lay prone on the soft leather sofa in his New York City penthouse. Lying flat was the only way for him to get relief from the constant nagging pain in his hip.

He clutched his hand around his phone and instructed Siri to call his dad.

"I was just going to call you, H," Dad said. "I heard about the board meeting. Sounds like you shut Morehouse down pretty quickly."

Holden grimaced. The confrontation with Stanley had left him frustrated and feeling weak. "You must have talked to Marjorie."

Dad chuckled. "That I did. She said you handled yourself well. I'm proud of you."

Holden warmed to his dad's praise. "Thanks, Dad. We still haven't recovered from David's theft. I'm glad you suggested selling the Texas property."

"It's a good move. Check your email when you get a chance. I forwarded a proposal to you for another project. It's a senior living development in Hornell, close to Almond Lake. Beautiful views and a pastoral setting."

"Does the proposal include any comps? Is it something we'd want to hold onto after it's built?"

"I'll leave those decisions to you. You are the CEO, after all."

"Whatever, Dad. You know you won't be able to resist putting in your two cents." Holden adjusted his position as the ibuprofen he'd taken kicked in. "How's Mom?"

"Why don't you ask her yourself?"

Holden imagined his dad passing the phone to Mom.

"Hi, honey." Mom's upbeat voice sounded through the phone. "How are you feeling?"

Holden's eyes burned with tears. Mom always asked about his health. Her positive attitude was one of the things keeping him hopeful during the long chemo and radiation treatments. That and his and his family's unwavering faith in God.

"I'm okay," Holden said, using one hand to press on his eyes. "Still some pain and stiffness."

"Are you keeping up with physical therapy?"

"Of course. Swimming, weights, blah blah blah."

"Don't get smart with me," Mom scolded. "Now, tell me what else is new."

Holden's thoughts swerved to his new next-door neighbor. Kayleigh had invaded his thoughts more than he wanted to admit. But if he mentioned her to his mother, she'd be ordering 'save the date' cards before he could count to three.

"Not much, Mom. I'm sure Dad brought you up to speed on the board meeting. Other than that, I'm looking for a temporary admin until Donna is able to come back to work."

"I sent her some flowers," Mom said. "You might think about sending her a gift card for some meal delivery."

Holden cringed. Donna had always taken care of

things like online ordering, etc. Perhaps his new admin could do it. If she accepted his offer, that is. He'd been pretty blunt with her, but that was his way. Especially with the constant pain in his hip.

"Holden? Are you still there?" Mom asked.

"I'm here. I'll take care of it. I'll let you go. Tell Dad I'll call him after I've looked at the proposal he sent."

"I love you," Mom said as she disconnected.

Holden let his hand drop to the floor. What would he do without his parents? Their marriage was rock solid, unlike so many of his wealthy peers.—men his dad's age, divorcing their aging wives and remarrying a newer, younger model. To his knowledge, his dad had never even looked at another woman.

At least Holden had concluded the conversation with his mom before she could bring up her favorite subject. When was he going to settle down and give him grandkids? He and his brother cringed whenever Mom brought up the subject.

Speaking of, Holden hadn't talked to Andrew in days.

Andrew picked up after three rings. "Hey, bro. How's life in the family dynasty?"

"Ahhh, so good. Sure you don't want to join me?"

Andrew laughed. "No way. As the oldest, you get the privilege of inheriting the responsibility."

"How's life in the slow lane?" Holden asked.

He pictured his brother lounging on the deck of his fishing boat in the middle of Keuka Lake.

"Beautiful. I just dropped off a bunch of tourists, and now, I'm kicking back with a glass of some local vino."

"Sounds like business is good." Holden felt a pang of jealousy. Andrew's fish chartering business kept him busy all summer and out in the open air.

"You should come out sometime. You haven't been on the boat since ..." Andrew's voice faded.

Holden didn't know who was more devastated, Andrew or him, at his cancer diagnosis.

"I will. Soon. Why don't you come up here for a visit? There's someone I want you to meet."

He'd get Andrew's take on his sexy neighbor and let him know if Holden was acting crazy.

"A woman, I hope. Yeah, I can come up in a couple of days. I'll check my schedule and text you."

"Great." Holden disconnected. Excitement built at seeing his brother. As kids, they'd been inseparable. As adults, they'd taken different career paths, but remained close.

Andrew would give his honest opinion about Kayleigh and her ability to do his admin work. He'd head back to his lake house first thing tomorrow.

Chapter 6

Kayleigh donned a floppy sun hat and snapped on the dogs' leashes. The hat kept the sun off most of her face. The bit of sun she'd gotten yesterday had brought her freckles out in force. The curse of being Irish and light-skinned.

She headed down the Donaldson's sloping grassy yard to a gate at the end of the property. Sandra had, of course, recorded the gate code in her bound instructions. Kayleigh led the dogs through the gate and down a dirt path to the water's edge.

The midmorning sun glinted off the lake's surface. The sun's rays bounced off the water, creating a dazzling display of glittering diamonds. Gentle lapping of the water against the shore was accompanied by the honking of Canada geese and the distant hum of a motorboat as it glided across the lake's surface. The fresh, crisp scent of the water filled the air, mingling with the aroma of sun-warmed earth.

Kayleigh let the dogs off-leash and watched in amusement as they danced from the water back to where she stood. She envied their total abandon to the moment. Rocky and Luna had no worries about their future.

When this dog and house-sitting gig was over, she'd return to Nashville with a pocketful of money and a heart full of dreams. The guy she talked to said she needed nine songs to cut a record. She had seven she was happy with. Surely she could get two more written during this gig.

"Luna, Rocky, come," Kayleigh called. The sun warmed her arms and legs and brought sweat trickling down her back.

She snapped on their leashes and walked them back through the gate and into the Donaldson's yard. Once they were released, they dashed across the yard and stood panting by the back door.

"I agree," Kayleigh said, dragging in a lungful of thick air. She glanced at the hole in the hedge toward the aqua blue water of Holden's swimming pool. He was in New York, right? Who would know if she took a quick dip in the inviting water?

Before she could talk herself out of it, Kayleigh dashed into the house, freshened the dog's drinking water, and changed into her swimsuit.

She paused at the edge of the property line and bit her lip. She composed a text to Holden.

Kayleigh: I accept your offer.

Her phone showed the bubbles as Holden typed a response.

Holden: Good. We will discuss details tomorrow.
Kayleigh: When will you be back from the City?
Holden: This afternoon

Kayleigh breathed a sigh of relief and strode the rest of the way through the hedge and to the pool. Her only thought was to cool off and get out before the guys showed up to repair the fence.

The water instantly chilled her hot skin. She walked down the pool steps and swam a couple of laps before pausing under the waterfall cascading down a rock wall at the deep end.

Too bad the Donaldson's didn't have a pool. She'd tell Holden pool privileges would have to be part of her employment agreement.

She climbed out of the pool, dried off, and returned to the Donaldson's.

"Want to go out?" she asked the sleeping dogs.

Luna raised her head, opened her mouth in a huge yawn, and went back to sleep.

"Too hot for you?" Kayleigh didn't blame them. High humidity and a cloudless day meant staying inside.

"I'll be in the living room." As if the pups cared.

Kayleigh changed out of her swimsuit and returned to the living room with her guitar and a notepad. Time to work on her new song. Something about being broken on the inside. Which brought her thoughts back to Holden.

Why had the check and the business card read Holden Holdings. Was the company named after him? But wasn't the company started by Holden's grandfather?

She set the guitar aside and pulled her laptop onto her knees. The Google search was still in her browsing history.

Yup, Grandfather Jeffries had started the company back in the fifties. Why not name it Jeffries Holdings?

Kayleigh typed 'Holden Jeffries III illness' into the search. One article came up. Kayleigh clicked on the link and read with growing horror the story of Holden's cancer battle.

That explained his crankiness.

Holden set his phone on the kitchen counter with a smile. He had a new administrative assistant. Of course, Kayleigh couldn't turn down his generous offer of double what she was getting from the Donaldsons. Money always talked louder than words.

His phone chirped with a notification from the security system at the house on Seneca Lake. The motion sensor picked up activity in the backyard. Holden opened the app, expecting to see the arrival of the yard guys to work on the fence.

His breath caught. He'd recognize that flaming red hair anywhere. At this moment, the head was attached to a curvy woman stepping out of his pool. The one-piece swimsuit clung to her body in ways that filled his mouth with cotton.

Flee youthful lusts.

Holden closed the app when the Bible verse from his childhood flashed into his brain. When normal thought returned, he asked himself why Kayleigh was using his pool. She had no right.

Time to get home and set some boundaries.

The car service dropped Holden off at his front door.

"Thanks, Henry," Holden said, climbing out of the back seat with his satchel.

"Need help, sir?"

"No, thank you." Holden shifted his cane to his left hand and used his right to carry the satchel. A white pickup sat to one side of the driveway bearing the logo of his landscape maintenance company. Holden hadn't realized they'd arrived since he'd turned off the motion-sensing app.

The inside of the house was a welcome relief from the heat. Holden limped upstairs and stripped off his dress shirt and slacks and put on a pair of shorts and a moisture-wicking golf shirt.

Downstairs, he stepped outside and walked to where the workmen stood.

Not working.

The two young men were leaning on their shovels, smiling and laughing, talking with someone beyond the fence.

Kayleigh.

He stepped closer to listen.

"How 'bout when we're done here you join us for a cold beer?"

"How about when you're done, I give you the check Mr. Jeffries left for you?"

"Ah, come on, pretty lady. You must be lonely in that big ole house all by your lonesome."

Holden heard Kayleigh's laugh.

"I have a couple of dog to keep me company."

"Dogs? That ain't no company. Come with us and we'll show you a good time."

Holden's blood pressure rose. "What do you think you're doing?" he demanded.

The two young workers whirled to face him.

"Uh, we're working on your repair," the one with a scraggly beard said.

"Get back to work and quit flirting." Holden stepped closer and spied Kayleigh standing on the other side of the broken fence. "You," he said. "Come with me."

Holden didn't wait to see if Kayleigh followed. His annoyance spread from the two guys to her. She'd likely encouraged them by engaging in their banter. He squashed the question why it bothered him so much.

Kayleigh's flip flops slapped against the pool deck behind him. Holden paused at the back door, allowing her to precede him into the house.

"Wow," she murmured. "I didn't realize how big your place is when I was here before."

Holden tried to see his home through Kayleigh's eyes. White wicker furniture held colorful cushions. The arrangement made the most of the view to Seneca Lake. Beyond the sunroom was a living room with wood plank flooring. The kitchen and breakfast nook created an open feel despite the abundance of wood paneling. Kayleigh followed him through the room and into the foyer.

"Let's go upstairs," he said. "Unless you're worried I'll take advantage of you."

Kayleigh shook her head with a smirk. "I'm pretty sure I can outrun you."

The comment stung. Holden cursed again the cancer that had stolen his vigor.

He'd converted the loft into an office because it was closest to the master bedroom. He pointed to one of the chairs facing his desk. "Sit."

Holden noted the freckles on Kayleigh's nose and cheeks. They stood out like Rorschach splotches on a white piece of paper. His fingers itched to trace a

pattern on her cheeks.
  Best to remain annoyed instead of attracted.

JANE DALY

Chapter 7

Kayleigh swallowed her irritation at being told to sit like she was one of the Donaldson's canines. If Holden was serious about paying double what she was being paid to house and dog sit, she'd leave New York with a nice pile of cash. Enough to finish paying music producer *and* get an apartment. If she could stand to work with the man standing in front of her. Right now, she wanted to tell Holden where he could take his job offer.

"I get fifteen hundred a week from the Donaldsons," Kayleigh said without preamble.

Holden lowered himself into the leather chair behind his desk. He pinned her with his gaze. "I'll confirm that with Robert."

"You do that." Kayleigh couldn't help the sarcasm creeping into her voice. This guy was insufferable. He'd been rude to the harmless flirting by guys doing the work on the fence. If it wasn't for the money, she'd tell him *see-ya*.

"Why were you in my pool earlier?"

Kayleigh sucked in a breath. Had he been home the whole time? A hot flush worked its way from her neck to her cheeks. A simple answer would be best.

"It was hot."

"Indeed." Holden's one word answer did nothing to calm her racing pulse.

"I'm sorry." Kayleigh lowered her gaze to escape Holden's piercing blue eyes. She picked a loose thread in her shorts. "Do you think I could use the pool once in a while? I am going to be working for you, after all." Her glaze flicked up and back down.

"Perhaps."

Kayleigh wanted to leap across the desk and strangle the man. She pressed her lips together to keep from saying something unbecoming.

Holden's cane dropped to the floor with a clatter. Kayleigh jumped.

"Let's discuss the terms of your temporary employment here," Holden said, ignoring his cane.

Finally.

"I will need you to work around my schedule. Do you think you can do that and take care of the Donaldson's pets?"

Kayleigh nodded without speaking.

"Give me your phone number so I can text you as needed."

She pulled her phone from her pocket. "I already sent you a text agreeing to work."

Holden had his own phone out. "So you did. What is your email?"

Kayleigh sent it to him via text. His next question hit her like a Tennessee tornado.

Holden rested his elbows on the desk. "You aren't pregnant, are you?"

Kayleigh gasped. Did she look pregnant? She glanced down at her tummy.

"No."

"Do you plan to get pregnant in the next six weeks?"

Kayleigh sprang to her feet and scowled. "That is none of your business. How dare you."

Holden rubbed a hand over the light stubble on his cheeks. "I apologize. My admin, Donna, had to take a leave because she's pregnant and on bed rest. I don't want to have to train you, and then, you leave."

Kayleigh stared at Holden through narrowed eyes.

Holden continued. "Please sit. I promise not to ask any more personal questions."

Kayleigh struggled between wanting to toss something at Holden's head before stomping out of the room and returning to the chair and having the opportunity to make a pile of cash.

She sat. "Fine."

"Fine," Holden echoed. "Come over tomorrow around ten, and I'll get you access to my computer, email, and Dropbox."

"Should I come to the front door?"

A ghost of a smile lifted Holden's lips. "When your *friends* are finished outside, there'll be a temporary gate between our two houses. When the Donaldsons return, I'll replace it with a regular fence."

Her *friends*? Sheesh.

"Sounds good." Kayleigh stood. "One more thing. I want my first week of pay up front. I don't want to slave for you and have you tell me you aren't satisfied with my work."

"Cash, Venmo, or …"

Kayleigh took a minute to answer. Was it possible he had that much cash lying around? If it wasn't for

Sandra's need for a last-minute replacement for their regular dog-sitter, she'd be lucky to find a dollar bill in a coat pocket.

"Venmo."

"Send me your Venmo info, and I'll take care of it tonight."

"Fine." She was saying that a lot. "I'll see you tomorrow." She turned to go but stopped at the door. "Think about the pool access."

Kayleigh thought she heard him chuckle as she strode from the room.

Holden inhaled the lingering scent of lavender left behind in Kayleigh's wake. She'd be a great replacement for Donna. It was apparent she could give as good as she got. He needed someone with a thick skin who wouldn't be offended by his abruptness.

His phone pinged with a text as he bent down to retrieve his cane.

Andrew: I will arrive tonight. I'll be hungry.

Holden: What time?

Andrew: Nine-ish. Make it Thai.

He was tempted to text Kayleigh and request she order their meal. But first, he needed to send her the money. After he checked with Robert and Sandra to confirm how much they were paying Kayleigh. Since David's betrayal, Holden didn't trust anyone.

Holden sent a quick text to Robert, explaining the situation and asking if there was a problem if Kayleigh split her time between the dogs and his needs.

He replayed their conversation in his head, remembering how red Kayleigh's face had gotten when he called her out about using his pool. He really didn't care that she'd used it. It had been worth it to see her dripping wet and clad in a swimsuit.

Speaking of, Holden went into his bedroom and changed into his swim trunks. Time for some physical therapy of the saltwater kind.

The Thai food arrived as Andrew climbed out of his Land Rover.

"Good timing, bro," Andrew said, handing the Uber Eats driver a tip.

Holden held the front door open. "Glad you made it before the food got cold."

They gave each other an awkward hug, Holden trying not to smack his brother with the cane, and Andrew trying to negotiate his overnight bag and the sack containing the food.

Andrew tossed his bag in the direction of the stairs and followed Holden to the dining room.

"I'm starved," he said.

"Me too."

While they inhaled the spicy meal, Holden brought Andrew up to speed on the recent board meeting and on his interactions with Kayleigh.

"She'll be here tomorrow to get started. You can meet her then." Holden frowned at Andrew's grin.

"I'd love to meet your new assistant."

"No way, Drew. Hands off." His brother's charm with the opposite sex was legendary. He left a string of broken hearts from Maine to Florida.

"No even a mild flirtation?" Andrew asked.

The thought of Andrew with Kayleigh brought a

flash of annoyance.

"No." He'd have to examine that thought later.

Andrew pretended outrage. "Why do you dangle a beautiful woman in front of me and then tell me hands off?"

"I never said she was beautiful."

"You didn't have to."

Holden sent his brother a closed-mouth smile. His twin knew him too well.

The next morning, Holden's phone pinged at nine forty-five.

Kayleigh: Should I go around to the front door?

Holden: The sliding door in the back will be open. Come upstairs to my office

She sent a thumbs up emoji.

Holden had fifteen minutes to swallow some ibuprofen and finish getting dressed. What used to be a thirty-minute morning routine now took more than an hour.

Stretching exercises, Vitamin E oil on the scar, and struggling to put on a pair of pants should get easier with time. At least, that's what his doctor said.

The sarcoma diagnosis had come out of nowhere. Cancer didn't run in his family. At least the situation made his brother more conscious of his health.

Speaking of his brother, Andrew must be sleeping in. His day usually began at dawn to take advantage of the early morning fishing. Good. Andrew wouldn't be able to flirt with Holden's new admin.

Chapter 8

Kayleigh kept an eye on the time while tossing a rubber ball for the Huskies to chase. They grappled over control of the ball before returning to her side, panting. Their tongues lolled out of the corners of their mouths, saliva dripping onto the wood deck.

"Ew, gross." The ball was slippery in her hand. "I'll need a shower after this," she told them.

When they were out of breath and their sides heaved from the exertion, Kayleigh let them into the house and refreshed their water bowls.

"I need to change clothes," she told them, staring down at her slobber-covered shorts.

She sent a quick text to Holden. He'd said to come to the back door. Nerves fluttered in her stomach at the thought of working side by side with him. His presence made her pulse increase, and not just from annoyance. There was something about the man that intrigued her. How had someone so young contracted cancer? Had he always been a cranky pants?

According to Samantha, he hadn't given off that vibe when she'd met him at a fund-raising gala.

Oh, well. Time to head over to the lion's den. And hope to not get devoured.

Kayleigh paused by Holden's swimming pool, remembering the first time she'd seen him, coming out of his pool dripping wet.

Rein it in, girl. You are not in the market for attraction.

Kayleigh headed to Holden's sliding glass door with a wry smile. The door slid open with barely a whisper. She took a moment to admire again the beauty of his home. Now that she'd been here twice, the heavy wood paneling on the walls and ceiling didn't feel quite so confining.

Kayleigh climbed up the stairs praying as she ascended. Prayers for patience. Not her best attribute. And a prayer for Holden to get some pain relief.

As she entered Holden's office area, she spied the back of his head. He sat in his desk chair facing out the windows banking the room.

"Ahem." She cleared her throat to get his attention.

The chair swung around. "Good morning," he said. "Are you ready to get started?"

Kayleigh narrowed her eyes. He looked like Holden, and sounded like Holden, but this guy sitting at Holden's desk, was *not* Holden. He'd never mentioned he had a twin, the skunk.

Fine, she'd play this guy's game. "Good morning, Boss."

"Have a seat," he said, motioning to one of the chairs facing the desk.

She remained standing. "You got some sun while you were gone," Kayleigh commented. His face was a few shades darker than Holden's.

He laughed. Yeah, definitely not Holden.

"Yes, I did. Get some sun. And how are you

today?"

"I'm fine." Kayleigh walked around the desk and leaned against it within a few inches of the man's leg. "More than fine, actually, now that I'm here." She sent him a seductive smile.

His eyebrows shot up and he grinned. "Okay."

"What's going on here?" Holden's angry voice interrupted whatever the guy was going to say.

Kayleigh jerked and stood upright. The man sitting at Holden's desk laughed.

"Not a thing, H. Not yet anyway." He grinned at Kayleigh.

She felt a hot flush on her cheeks. Her attempt at teasing Holden's brother backfired big-time.

"I warned you, Andrew," Holden said, limping toward them.

Kayleigh's eyes narrowed. Holden had warned his brother about her? What was that supposed to mean?

Andrew stood and raised his hands in surrender. "You'll be happy to know she can tell the difference between us. I'll bet my boat she'd never tried to flirt with *you*."

Holden scowled. "Get lost, Drew. I have work to do."

Andrew sent her one last cheeky grin before he strode out of the room. Holden sat behind the desk and motioned Kayleigh over.

"I've unlocked my laptop so you can have access. I need you to find the email from my dad and print out the attachment he sent. Make two copies. Look through my unread emails and delete all the junk and spam. If there's anything you think needs my attention, print it out. Think you can do that?"

Kayleigh bristled under his condescending tone. "I think my little ole pea brain can do that."

"After you're done, bring everything down to the sunroom."

Kayleigh nodded, grateful he made no mention of the way she'd leaned toward his brother with a coy smile.

"Any questions?" Holden said, pushing himself to his feet using the desk for support.

"Why is your company Holden Holdings and not Jeffries Holdings?"

Holden gave an exasperated sigh. "My grandfather named it after his great grandmother's maiden name. He thought it sounded more professional."

"Ah. Thanks for clearing that up."

"Anything else?"

"Where's the printer?"

Holden used his cane to point to one of the wall-to-wall cabinets on one side of the room. He limped toward the hall, leaning heavily on his cane.

Kayleigh watched him go, alternating between annoyance and sympathy. She had a feeling Holden wouldn't want to know she had either of those emotions.

She fanned herself with one hand. So, Holden was a twin. How could two men be so devastatingly handsome? So not fair. Andrew had seemed surprised she could tell the difference between them.

"I'll bet they tormented teachers back in the day," she murmured.

Holden's email showed fifty-two unread emails. It felt weird to read someone else's mail, but she did as Holden had instructed. After deleting the junk ones, she took time to read each one to determine if it was something requiring Holden's immediate attention.

Why did he want them printed? Seemed odd. With a shrug, she printed the ones she deemed important and scrolled down to the email he'd said his dad sent. The proposal was over thirty pages long. And he wanted two copies? How many trees had to die to make Holden happy?

While the proposal printed, Kayleigh read through the pages. It outlined a development in Hornell for a senior living facility. She'd grown up in Hornell, and her parents still lived there. The artist's rendition of the place looked impressive. It might be a great alternative for Granny, who'd moved in with her folks when Kayleigh left for Nashville.

She gathered up the printed pages, stapled the two proposals, and carried the stack downstairs.

Holden descended the stairs one step at a time. His anger toward Andrew grew at each step. He found his brother lounging on one of the wicker chairs in the sunroom, a can of soda in one hand.

"What did I tell you about flirting with my new assistant?"

Andrew chuckled. "She started it."

"Doubtful."

"I can assure you she knew I wasn't you the minute she stepped into the room, H."

Holden had lost count of the number of times Andrew had swooped in and stolen a girl from him, pretending to be him. Thankfully, those days were long past, and the fights they'd gotten into had turned into mutual respect. Thank God for adulthood.

Except...

What had his brother been about to say to Kayleigh? He glared at Andrew, his face a mirror of his own.

Holden sank onto one of the brightly-colored cushions with a grunt.

"How's the hip?" Andrew asked.

Holden shrugged. "Same. Hurts like H-E-double hockey sticks."

Andrew choked on a sip of soda as he tried not to laugh. "What are you, Amish? Nobody says that except little old ladies and people who refuse to use electricity."

Holden smiled despite himself. Hanging out with Andrew always lifted his spirits. "You may have a sailor's mouth, but I," he waved a finger in the air, "prefer to keep my language above reproach."

This time Andrew didn't hold back. His guffaw echoed against the wood ceiling. Holden joined him.

He leaned back and stretched his bad leg, laying it on the coffee table. "What do you think about my new admin? What does that amazing sixth sense tell you?"

Andrew closed his eyes and leaned his head back. "Well, she *is* gorgeous."

"But can she do the job?"

"Who cares?"

Holden shook his head. "Not helpful, Drew."

Andrew opened his eyes. "I'd pay money just to stare at her."

"But can she do the job? What is your first impression?"

Andrew ticked off his comments with his fingers.

"First, she immediately knew I wasn't you. Second, she wasn't shy about making me uncomfortable. Third, I think you like her."

Holden shifted on the cushion. His twin's observations were usually right on. There was something about the beautiful Kayleigh that intrigued him. She was willing to go head-to-head with him, even when he was being a horse's rear end.

The woman they'd been discussing stepped into the room. Holden's head swiveled to take in her slow advance toward them. She held a sheaf of papers.

"I printed out two copies of the proposal like you asked. The emails are printed too. And I organized the emails into folders on your computer."

Holden held out his hand for the printed sheets. "Folders?"

"Urgent, not urgent, needs a response. You'll see."

Holden cut his gaze to Andrew, who straightened in his chair. He knew what Andrew was thinking. That Kayleigh was more than capable of doing the job.

Holden thumbed through the printed emails and tossed them on the coffee table. He handed Andrew one of the proposal copies. "Take a look at this and tell me what you think."

"You know I have no interest in the family business."

"I know. But I still want to hear what you have to say about this proposal. Dad seemed pretty excited about it."

Holden glanced at Kayleigh, who stood with her arms at her sides. Today, she wore the same denim skirt as the first time he'd seen her, including the cowboy boots. Her red hair spilled over the shoulders of the purple top that hugged her body. Andrew was right when he said he'd pay money just to stare at her. His pulse spiked when his thoughts shifted to seeing her in her swimsuit.

Best not to go there.

Kayleigh crossed her arms over her chest as if she were able to read his mind. "Anything else you need me to do?"

Holden cleared his throat. "In my list of contacts on the computer, you'll find the number for my pilot. His name is Steve Cantrell. Call him, identify yourself as my new admin, and tell him to be ready for wheels up day after tomorrow."

"Where are you going?"

"I'll fly to Thailand."

Kayleigh spun and headed back through the living room. Holden watched her mount the stairs until he could no longer see her.

Andrew gave a low whistle. "Wow."

Holden sent him a wry smile. "Yeah."

The brothers spent the next half-hour going through the proposal page by page.

Andrew rubbed a hand over his head. "I'd say go for it. Looks like the developer has covered all the bases." He yawned and stretched his arms over his head. "I'm going for a swim."

Holden was tempted to join his brother but opted to go upstairs and check on Kayleigh's progress. He found her sitting behind his desk, chatting on the phone, a huge smile on her face. He sat in one of the chairs facing the desk and listened to her side of the conversation. If this was a personal phone call, he'd let her know in no uncertain terms that wasn't allowed.

"I don't think so," Kayleigh said. "But thank you. That's quite an offer."

Holden cleared his throat to get Kayleigh's attention. She nodded in his direction and continued talking.

"Perfect. I'll let him know. I look forward to meeting you, too." Kayleigh disconnected and set the phone down.

"Who were you talking to?" he demanded.

Kayleigh's smile faded. "That was Steve. Your pilot. The one you told me to call."

Holden inwardly cringed. Why did he act like a tool with her? "And he will be ready day after tomorrow?"

Kayleigh's eyes narrowed and her finger beat a tattoo on the desk. "That's what you asked for."

"Of course. Well—" What he was going to say was interrupted by the doorbell.

"Want me to get that?" Kayleigh asked, getting to her feet.

"I will answer the door." Holden used his cane and the arm of the chair to stand. "Put the flight information into my calendar on my computer," he said, heading toward the top of the stairs. He descended the staircase to see who his unexpected visitor might be.

JANE DALY

Chapter 9

Kayleigh watched Holden limp to the stairs. She'd work this one week and then tell Holden where he could put this job. Since he'd already paid her for the week, she was obligated to take his abuse. But after that, the money he'd dangled wasn't worth the stress.

She'd much prefer getting to know Andrew. He looked fun. Maybe too fun. She'd had her share of guys who had no serious bone in their bodies. They wanted a good time, a quick hook-up, and then on to the next girl.

Kayleigh gritted her teeth and went to work transferring the notes she'd written about the flight and which airport Steve would be at onto Holden's calendar. Steve had provided the private car service Holden used, so Kayleigh used their online reservation system to order a pickup for Holden an hour before the flight. She put this information into Holden's calendar as well.

Satisfied she'd done all she could, Kayleigh closed the laptop and decided to tell Holden she needed to go next door and let the dogs out.

"Good morning, ma'am." The voice belonged to a

middle-aged woman wearing jeans and a T-shirt. She had a blue bandana covering her head and carried a cleaning tote in one hand.

"Morning," Kayleigh responded.

"You must be the new administrative assistant." She held out her hand for Kayleigh to shake.

"And you must be the housekeeper?"

"Going on two years," she responded.

Golly, this woman must be a saint to put up with Mr. Cranky Pants for two years.

"The gentlemen are on the back patio," she said. "I'm Tara."

"Nice to meet you. I'm Kayleigh."

Tara nodded and took the tote in the direction of the kitchen.

Kayleigh walked through the living room, sunroom, and stopped at the open sliding glass door. Holden stood with his arm around a tall blonde woman wearing a colorful maxi skirt and white tank.

Where did the flash of jealousy come from? Sure, Holden and his brother were drop-dead handsome. But she had no claim on either one. Maybe it was the easy smile on Holden's face as he looked at the woman tucked under his arm. Kayleigh stood to one side of the door to hear their conversation.

The woman wrapped her free arm around Andrew and pulled the guys in for a group hug. "I'm back from my trip to Florida, and I wanted to spend time with my two favorite people."

"It's so good to see you," Holden said. "I missed you." He dropped a kiss on the woman's head.

Kayleigh's heart fluttered. What would it be like to have him look at her with tenderness instead of the scowl he usually wore.

Song lyrics trickled in her brain.

You used to hold me like I was your treasure. Now you hold another and I'm on the outside looking in.

She stepped out the door, anxious to get back to the Donaldson's and work on a new song.

"Hello, who are you?" the woman asked, pulling away from Holden's arm.

Holden's arms dropped to his sides. "This is my temporary admin, Kayleigh. She's taking Donna's place for a few weeks."

The woman took a few steps toward Kayleigh. "How great you could fill in. I keep telling Holden he relies too much on Donna." She held out her hand. "I'm Jenna."

"Kayleigh," she replied. She glanced at Holden. "I'm heading home. I need to let the dogs out."

The scowl was back on Holden's face. "Fine. I'll text you if I have any questions."

"Nice to meet you," Kayleigh said to Jenna. "And you," she added, glancing at Andrew. He replied with a smile and a half-bow.

Kayleigh felt three pair of eyes on her back as she stepped into the planter and through the gate. She caught a bit of Jenna's question about the gate in the hedge, but didn't slow down to hear Holden's response. She needed to get away from the Jeffries brothers and Holden's girlfriend.

Good thing she wasn't looking for a summer romance, she reminded herself. She was here to dog sit and write music.

Luna and Rocky were waiting by the back door when Kayleigh strode up the deck stairs to the back door. She let them out and opened up the instruction booklet Sandra had left. The dog groomer would be at the house in an hour and a half. Kayleigh had just enough time to jot down some lyrics before he arrived.

But first, she sent a text to the music producer she'd contracted with.

I'm working on my songs. Should have three more in a week or so.

The message showed it was delivered, but no bubbles appeared indicating an answer. If she didn't get some decent songs written by the end of September, she'd lose the deposit she'd given to Gary Golden, the music producer. The contract she'd signed, along with most of her hard-earned savings, was clear. A total of nine songs must be written, put to music, and accepted by September 30.

Time to get writing. Kayleigh couldn't afford to lose her deposit.

"She seems nice," Jenna said, dropping onto a deck chair in the shade.

Holden clenched his teeth when Andrew responded.

"Super nice. But Holden won't let me near her."

Jenna laughed. "Because you have a wicked reputation, Drew."

"Yeah, but H doesn't have a claim on her," Andrew said with a mock pout.

"Not yet," Jenna said. "But I saw the way you looked at her, H."

Holden sank onto a chair on the opposite side of the table. "Why are you here, Jenna?"

Jenna put a hand on her chest in mock affront.

"Why can't I spend some time with my brothers?"

Holden frowned. "Because you never go anywhere without an ulterior motive."

"Okay, fine. Mom told me to check out your new admin. She is anxious for one of us to get hitched and …" she wagged a finger and mimicked their mother's voice, "'give me some grandchildren.'"

Jenna looked at Andrew. "That's not gonna happen for you, Drew. You are a serial dater."

"Not gonna happen for me, either," Holden said. Who would want to marry a man who was incapable of having children? Sure, the doctors said he *might* have some sperm that didn't die during radiation. But no woman wanted to take a chance on something that *might* happen.

Andrew wandered over and smacked Holden on the shoulder. "I think it's time to get our sister hooked up with someone. Then the pressure will be on her and not us."

"I agree," Holden said.

Jenna was already shaking her head. "No way. I have zero interest in the dating scene. I'm into my career."

"What career?" Holden and Andrew said in unison.

"Come on, guys, you know I'm getting my reputation established as an event coordinator."

Holden exchanged a glance with his brother. They both burst out laughing.

Jenna scraped back her chair. "If you two are going to be juvenile, I'm going in the house to unpack."

"Unpack?" Holden asked with alarm. "How long are you staying?"

Jenna patted him on the shoulder as she passed his

chair. "Just overnight. Or longer. Don't worry, I won't get in the way of you and your new admin." She sent him a grin which set Holden's teeth on edge. Having two siblings was annoying.

Chapter 10

Kayleigh sat back and surveyed the work she'd accomplished on her newest song. Her scribbled notes and hastily prepared music sheets lay strewn on the kitchen table. The pups snoozed in their oversized beds in the corner of the room.

"What'd you think, guys?" Kayleigh smiled when Luna and Rocky responded with a couple of tail thumps.

"Not impressed? Well, wait till you hear my best song ever."

Kayleigh set her guitar on the table and wandered to the living room to stare out the window. From her vantage point, she could watch for the groomer's van coming up the driveway. Tall American basswood trees lined the drive, their odd-shaped leaves leaving Rorschach-like shadows on the sprawling lawn.

What would it be like to live in such luxury? Surrounded by unimaginable wealth, able to purchase anything she wanted. Kayleigh sank onto the padded window seat and rested her chin in her palm.

Her wants were simple. A place to live, the ability to write songs, and friends who loved her and cared about her. The only thing missing was the love of a man.

Kayleigh envied her parents. Despite her mother's hovering over her only child, her folks had been married for over thirty years. Happily married. They had something most of her friends didn't.

A white van with the words Kendrick's Kritters rumbled up the driveway and jerked to a stop in front of the porch. Kayleigh didn't have to call Luna and Rocky. Their toenails clicked on the wood floor as they dashed to the front door and stood at attention.

"Ah, you recognize the groomer, do you?" she asked, patting them on the head. The minute she opened the front door, they sprang out and greeted the groomer as she climbed out of the van.

"Hi, guys," she greeted the squirming dogs. "Who wants to go first?"

"Hi, I'm Kayleigh," Kayleigh said, stepping toward the woman.

"Where's Dee Dee?" the woman asked.

"I'm filling in for her. Sandra said she had a family emergency."

The woman seemed to take this in. "I'm Anna. I guess Sandra has given you detailed instructions on what my schedule for Luna and Rocky is." She smiled.

Kayleigh smiled back, sharing the joke. "Oh, yes. Quite detailed."

"Well, let's get started. I have a busy schedule today." She leaned down and spoke to the dogs. "Who's first?"

"Want me to drag one of them back into the house?" Kayleigh asked.

"That'd be great." Anna grasped the collar of the pup closest to her, Rocky. "Come on, Rocky Raccoon.

Let's hop into the van."

Kayleigh pulled a whining Luna away and dragged her to the front door. "Don't worry about knocking when you're done. Come on in."

"Will do."

Kayleigh closed the front door. "Let's get you a treat, girl." Luna stopped tugging against Kayleigh's arm and trotted into the kitchen. Once she'd gotten her treat, Luna returned to the front door and lay down with her head resting on her paws.

Kayleigh smiled. What great dogs. Maybe when she was an established song writer in Nashville, she'd get a pet.

In the meantime, a song niggled at the edges of her brain. She hurried to the table to start writing.

I ain't no French-tipped champagne kinda girl
Won't take your Tesla Maserati to make my head twirl
Just give me blue jeans, porch swings bare feet
Give me a song with a good ole country beat

Don't want no 5 star 5 carat up town
Won't wear no high heels high fashion designer gown
Just give me blue jeans, porch swings bare feet
Give me a song with a good ole country beat

The sound of the front door opening interrupted Kayleigh's flow.

"It's just me," Anna called.

A moment later, Rocky bounded into the kitchen and thrust his wet nose at Kayleigh's arm.

"You want a treat, don't you?" Kayleigh stood and retrieved a dog treat for the newly groomed pup. "You look beautiful, Mr. Rocky," she said, running her hand down Rocky's sleek back. Anna had done an amazing job ridding him of excess fur and trimming it close to his body. As soon as Rocky was happily settled on his bed, Kayleigh returned to the table. Goosebumps broke out on her arms as she looked at what she'd written.

Talk about a contrast between where she was staying and her roots. Simple pleasures, feeling the soft grass tickle the bottoms of her feet, listening to country music in the back of a pickup while staring up at the sky.

She sighed, longing for the life before she decided to break into the music industry. But this song … this could be the one. With a Carrie Underwood or Kelly Pickler vibe, this one song might be her golden ticket.

Kayleigh grabbed her phone and sent another text to Gary Golden, the music producer.

Kayleigh: Wait till you hear the one I'm working on. I hope you'll be as excited as I am.

She set the phone on the table and penned a few more lyrics.

> *Keep your two dozen two carat high class*
> *Give me moonshine whiskey in a plastic glass*
> *Don't need no Garth Brooks front row Instagram*
> *I'd rather dance in the park with a country band*
> *Walk home in the dark holding hands*
> *Give me blue jeans, porch swings, bare feet*
> *Give me a song with a good ole country beat*

Her attention was grabbed by a ping from her

phone.
Your text could not be sent. Try again?
That was weird. Kayleigh hit 'try again' and waited.
Your text could not be delivered.
Her pulse spiked. She jabbed Gary's number into the phone to call him.

"The number you have reached is not in service at this time."

No, no, no. This couldn't be happening. Where was Gary Golden? Where was the five thousand dollars she'd paid him?

The next morning, Holden hugged his brother before Andrew climbed off the dock and into his boat.

"Who brought your boat here?" Holden asked. The morning sun glinted off the smooth surface of the lake.

Andrew's grin split his face. "A friend."

Holden took a minute to study his brother's face. "Who is she?"

Andrew's face reddened. "My friend Laura and her brother dock their boat near mine."

"You're like a chick magnet," Holden said.

Andrew shrugged. "I can't help it if I'm ruggedly handsome."

Holden shook his head with a chuckle. It was true. Andrew attracted women like ants to honey. Why couldn't he attract one lovely redhead?

Try smiling once in a while.

Holden rubbed a hand over his chest. Yeah, like *that* would work.

"I'm leaving my Rover here for a couple of days," Andrew said. "Please don't go joyriding."

"As if," Holden said, brandishing his cane in his brother's direction. "Take care, Drew," he said, watching with a twinge of jealousy as Andrew nimbly hopped onto his boat.

"You, too, H." Andrew pulled on a stained ball cap and gave Holden a mock salute. The motor rumbled to life and Andrew began the slow reverse into the lake.

Holden longed for the days when he and Andrew ran like wild animals around their parents' property—with Jenna always trying to keep up. The three were only minutes apart in age, but the twins didn't want their sister to play with them.

Though triplets in reality, Holden and Andrew were identical twins. Statistically, multiple births like theirs were rare. Twins in one sac and another baby in an additional sac. The three of them were always close, but he and Drew had that shared DNA thing.

Andrew paused the boat and called over his shoulder, "Go for the girl, H!" He gunned the motor before Holden could respond. Not even Andrew knew of Holden's potential sterility. How could he be a man without that?

He made his way up the slope to the back deck and found Jenna lounging in a chair with a steaming cup of coffee.

"How long are you planning to stay?" Holden asked, taking a seat next to her. He gazed down to where he could just barely glimpse Andrew's boat bouncing along the surface of Seneca Lake.

"Didn't Mom ever tell you it's rude to ask guests how long they're staying? It makes it sound like you want me to leave."

Holden quirked a brow at her.

Jenna smacked him on the arm. "Stop. You know you love me and can't stand to be apart."

"Hmm."

Jenna shook her head with a wry smile. "I'll be out of your hair tomorrow, big brother." She took a sip of coffee and regarded him over the rim.

Holden frowned. "I can't read your mind like I can Drew's, but I know you're plotting in that beautiful head of yours."

As soon as the words left his mouth, Kayleigh stepped through the hedge. "Good morning," she greeted them. Holden noticed the absence of her usual smile. Her eyes were puffy and red, and her cheeks were stiff.

Jenna raised her cup of coffee in a salute. "Morning, neighbor. Want some coffee?"

Kayleigh reached the table where Holden and Jenna sat. "I better not." Holden caught her glance as she asked, "What do you want me to do today?"

"I left a list on my desk."

She nodded. "Okay, then. I'll just get out of you and your girlfriend's hair."

Jenna choked on a sip of coffee and waved a hand in front of her face. "Girlfriend?" she sputtered.

Kayleigh's gaze cut between him and his sister. Holden glanced at Jenna and a laugh burst from both in unison. Kayleigh's face grew an adorable shade of pink.

Holden leaned forward and spoke to Jenna. "How many times have people assumed you and I or you and Andrew were a couple?"

Jenna's eyes twinkled. "Oh, at least a hundred and seven."

Kayleigh looked ready to cry. Holden's sympathy

for the woman caused his laughter to die. "Jenna is my sister. We're triplets. Me, Andrew, and Jenna."

"B-but how is that possible?" Kayleigh sputtered.

"I'll skip the statistical probabilities," Jenna said. "Basically, our mom produced two eggs at the same time, and both were fertilized. My two brothers are identical—"

"And Jenna here is the spare." Holden smiled fondly at his sister.

"I resent that," Jenna protested. "If you guys hadn't been so pushy, I might have been the oldest."

Kayleigh twisted her hands together. "I just assumed ..."

"Don't worry about it," Jenna said. "You're not the first."

"I better get to work," Kayleigh said.

Holden watched her step through the back door. He turned to find his sister watching him.

"What?" he demanded.

"You need to be nicer to her," Jenna said, shaking her finger at him.

"I'm nice," Holden said.

"You like her."

Jenna's statement brought him up short. He did like her, but he was sure the attraction wasn't mutual. Even if it was, why bother? Kayleigh would be gone in a few weeks, and he wasn't in the mood for a summer romance.

Jenna set her coffee mug on the table and pushed back her chair. "I'm going in the house."

"Stay out of my office," Holden warned. The last thing he wanted was for his sister to pester Kayleigh.

Jenna sent him a grin in response.

Chapter 11

Kayleigh dragged herself up the stairs to Holden's office. Could this day get any worse? She'd spent most of the night trying to find Gary Golden. His phone was disconnected, and her emails to him bounced back. Even his website was gone.

Gary Golden was a ghost who had disappeared with her money. Maybe it was time to let her dream of being a country songwriter die.

To add to her embarrassment, she thought Holden's sister was his girlfriend. Ugh. If she didn't have work to do, she'd go back to bed and pull the covers over her head.

Holden had left a detailed note on his desk for tasks he wanted done. She should have taken up Jenna's offer of coffee.

Kayleigh logged on to his computer and sorted through Holden's emails. Why did he want them printed? Seemed a waste when it would be just as easy for her to put them into folders. 'Not urgent,' 'Urgent,' and 'look at later.'

With a shrug, she checked that task off the list.

"Am I interrupting?" Jenna spoke from the other side of the loft. She approached and sat across the desk.

"Not really." Kayleigh studied Jenna's face for any resemblance to the Jeffries brothers. Holden and Andrew's hair was dark and their eyes blue. Jenna had blond hair and the same blue eyes. But her face was softer, and she didn't have that cute dimple in her chin.

"I hope you will forgive my brother for being grouchy. He didn't used to be this way. Since his cancer, his personality changed."

Forgive Mr. Cranky Pants? That was bit difficult. If it wasn't for the obscene amount of money he was paying her, she'd tell him *adios* in a hot minute.

When Kayleigh didn't respond, Jenna continued. "His cancer came out of nowhere. We all were devastated, Andrew especially. Those two ..." Jenna's voice trailed off.

"They seem close," Kayleigh commented.

"Oh, yes. Very."

"I'm an only child," Kayleigh said.

Jenna smiled. "When I was a kid, I would have envied you. Having two brothers, especially twin brothers, was a lot to handle. They tormented me endlessly. Either they ditched me to play by themselves, or they included me, and somehow, it turned into a prank. The joke was always on me."

Kayleigh felt her face relax as she watched Jenna's face crinkle into a grin. "Sounds brutal."

"Hashtag truth. Dealing with brothers will either break you or make you stronger."

Kayleigh shrugged. "I wouldn't know."

Jenna pushed herself to her feet. "Anyway, I wanted to let you know to give H a chance. He really is a good guy. And I think he likes you."

"Doubtful," Kayleigh said.

Jenna shook a finger at her. "Don't be fooled by his crusty exterior. He's like a toasted marshmallow, dark and crispy on the outside and gooey on the inside."

"Why are you telling me this? I'm just his temporary admin."

"You're totally different from the women he's dated. Unfortunately, our wealth seems to attract women, and men, who want our money more than a relationship. They'll do or say anything to drag us into their lives. You don't have that same vibe."

Kayleigh huffed through her nose. She was dead broke, living in a stranger's home, and had no other way to support herself. She was surprised that desperation wasn't oozing from her pores.

"I'm serious," Jenna said. "I want Holden to be happy. He needs to settle down, get married, and have a ton of kids."

"What about Andrew?"

Jenna laughed. "Getting Andrew to settle down would be like trying to grab a handful of Seneca Lake."

"I'm not looking for a boyfriend." Kayleigh turned her attention to Holden's computer, hoping to end the conversation.

"Sometimes, these things happen when you aren't looking." With that cryptic statement, Jenna glided from the room.

Kayleigh thought about her best friend, Samantha, and how she found true love with Logan, when she was in hiding from a stalker. Sam's modeling agency had rented the house next door to Logan's for a safe place for Sam to stay until the stalker was caught. Such a random set of circumstances.

Just like this one. Kayleigh pushed the chair back

and rubbed her face. Exhaustion pulled at her eyelids. Her head felt like it was stuffed with bubble wrap. If Holden liked her, he had a rotten way of showing it.

Holden stripped off his shirt and stepped into the pool. Using the handrail to steady him, he waded in unto he could float on his back.

His pain level had gone down in the past couple of days. But after the physical therapist came today, it would probably spike up to agonizing levels.

Instead of swimming laps, Holden used his arms to stay afloat, enjoying the feel of sun on his face. His thoughts turned to his sister. He loved Jenna to pieces, but her interference irritated him. Between her and Andrew, they'd have him engaged to Kayleigh before the week was up.

Sure, Kayleigh was easy on the eyes. She seemed intelligent enough to handle his administrative work. Her saltiness amused him. He could name on one hand the women who dared to challenge him. Mom, Jenna, and Donna.

In the past, he'd have calculated his moves, planned how he'd get and keep a woman's attention. But now, with this stupid cancer thing, he'd lost his mojo. The last thing Holden wanted was a woman's pity.

His phone pinged with a text and vibrated the waterproof Tag Heuer watch on his wrist. Holden pulled himself out of the pool and limped to the table.

Kayleigh: Anything else you need me to do

Holden dried his hands and arms before tapping out a response. Why didn't Kayleigh come down and ask him in person? *Because she doesn't like you.*

The thought gave him pause. Because he was curt and blunt with her.

Holden: No

He returned to the pool, but the pleasure he felt before Kayleigh's text had disappeared. He climbed out of the pool again, toweled off, and donned his shirt.

Before heading upstairs, Holden went to the kitchen and prepared a cup of coffee. He'd take it to Kayleigh as a peace offering. It was a challenge to carry the mug in one hand and his cane in the other. It rendered him unable to use the banister for support. The last thing he needed was to fall backwards and end up in a heap at the foot of the stairs.

Stupid cancer.

He found Kayleigh sitting behind his desk, staring at her phone.

"I brought you some coffee. Hope you like cream and sugar." Holden set the mug on a coaster on the desk.

"Thanks. I could use some more caffeine." Kayleigh lifted the mug to her nose and inhaled.

"I think you're supposed to drink it to get the desired effect."

Kayleigh laughed, and Holden's breath caught. Her laugh was unlike the shrill laughter of some of the women he'd dated. Hers didn't sound forced.

"Don't worry," Kayleigh said, bringing the mug to her lips. "This will go directly to my bloodstream." She took an appreciative sip.

Holden waited until she'd take a couple of drinks of the brew. "You looked a little stressed when you got here this morning. Is everything okay?"

Sweat broke out on the back of his neck when

Kayleigh's eyes filled with tears. Women's tears did him in.

"Everything is definitely not okay." Kayleigh fingered the tears from her eyes. "I did something stupid."

"Wait here," Holden said. He shuffled into his bedroom and changed out of his wet swim trunks and into a pair of soft sweats. He returned to the office and found Kayleigh resting her head on his desk. She snapped to attention when he sat down.

"What did you do that was stupid?" Holden hoped his voice carried concern.

Kayleigh regarded him with watery eyes. "I trusted someone I shouldn't have."

Boy, did he know how that felt. "How so?"

Kayleigh groaned. "Are you sure you want to hear this? I feel stupid."

"Go ahead."

"I met this guy, a music producer, and he said if I could come up with six to nine winning songs, he could get me a contract with a music label. I gave him money as a down payment for time at a music studio, once he approved my songs." She slapped her hands on his desk. "I can't believe I'm so stupid."

"Did you sign a contract with this music producer?"

"Yes. But a lot of good it does me now. He's a ghost."

"Can you hire a private investigator to find him?"

"Sure. With all my millions of dollars." Kayleigh looked ready to cry again. "Besides, even if he is found, there's no guarantee he will give me my money back."

"How much did you pay him?"

Kayleigh groaned. "Five grand. All my savings."

Holden sat back and regarded her. Five thousand dollars was walking around money in his world. But it was similar to what David had stolen. Five million to him was like five thousand to this woman.

"Remind me someday to tell you about the time I trusted someone, and it didn't turn out well."

Kayleigh drained her coffee and sat back in his big leather chair. "Sure."

"In the meantime, why don't you go home. You can finish this stuff up later." He waved a hand over the papers on his desk.

"Why are you flying to Thailand?" Kayleigh asked.

"Ah. Good question. I'm on the board of a nonprofit that rescues sex workers in Thailand and trains them to do other kinds of work. I'm going to check on the progress of our new women's dormitory."

"That sounds amazing."

Holden leaned forward. "It is. Very rewarding to see these women light up when they're given the chance to escape prostitution."

Kayleigh regarded him for a moment and stood. "Guess I'll go home, then."

Holden stood. "You're doing a good job. Thank you."

A ghost of a smile lifted the corners of Kayleigh's mouth. "How painful was that to say?"

Holden smiled despite himself. "Terribly."

JANE DALY

Chapter 12

Kayleigh cast a longing glance at Holden's pool as she made her way across the deck to the gate between his yard and the Donaldson's. Sweat gathered on the back of her neck. Maybe she'd ask if she could swim later.

In the meantime, she'd let the dogs out, play with them for a bit, and crawl under the covers of her amazingly soft bed.

Rocky and Luna were more than happy to run around the backyard, chasing each other and sniffing the bushes. They seemed impervious to the heat now that Anna had shaved back a lot of their fur. If only there was a way for her to be impervious to her circumstances.

Why had she let herself be cheated by Mr. Gary *snake-in-the-grass* Golden? She'd be beating herself up for weeks.

Holden had said he had a story too. His loss couldn't even be close to hers. She might have to abandon her dream of going back to Nashville. With the Donaldson's money and the money she'd make from Holden, Kayleigh could find a place to live, but she'd have to find a job and start completely over.

"I'm overwhelmed," she said out loud. Rocky nudged her hand with his nose. Kayleigh scratched his head until he pulled away to chase his sister again. If only she could be as carefree as a dog.

Her thoughts turned to Holden's sudden change of mood. He actually complimented her. 'You're doing a good job,' he'd said. And he'd returned her joke when she'd asked how painful it was for him to utter the words.

His smile had revealed straight white teeth. No doubt from expensive dental work. All three Jeffries siblings had beautiful smiles. But Holden ... Kayleigh had felt a rumble of nerves in her stomach when he smiled.

There was more to the man than met the eye. Gruff, irritable, yet involved with an international nonprofit helping sex workers escape the trade. If she was looking for a summer flirtation, Holden might be the Blake Shelton to her Gwen Stefani.

"That's stupid," Kayleigh said to Luna. Both dogs swarmed around her before making a beeline to the back door.

"Sure, let's go inside and out of this heat."

While Luna and Rocky slurped water from their bowls, Kayleigh retrieved a bottle of water from the subzero fridge and rolled it over her forehead before cracking it open.

Her phone buzzed with an incoming call from Samantha.

"Hey, bestie," Kayleigh said, carrying the phone into the living room. She plopped onto the cool leather sofa with a sigh.

"You sound beat," Sam said.

Kayleigh's eyes burned with unshed tears. "You won't believe what happened." She spilled the Gary Golden saga while tears leaked from her eyes.

"That's awful," Sam said. "Is there anything you can do? Any recourse?"

"Doubtful. He's a ghost." Kayleigh's stomach churned with a combination of anger and dismay.

"Oh, honey, I'm so sorry that happened. I was thinking of coming to visit you in a day or two. How does that sound?"

Kayleigh looked around the massive living room. The empty house echoed. "That would be great. The only interaction I've had is with Mr. Cranky Pants."

"How's that going?"

Kayleigh paused. Since Holden's unexpected compliment, she felt better about working for him. On the other hand, being in close proximity with him made her pulse spike. She'd have to watch herself to keep the attraction from growing into something unmanageable.

Sam's voice interrupted her train of thought. "You're taking a long time to answer."

Kayleigh sighed. "I'll tell you all about it when you get here. Send me a text when to expect you."

"Okay, girlfriend, but when I arrive, I want all the tea."

"You've got it." She disconnected and tossed the phone onto the opposite side of the sofa.

Kayleigh eyed her guitar she'd abandoned on the coffee table. "Not today, Marty." She'd named her Martin guitar the unimaginative name of Marty. "Not feeling inspired."

Time for some comfort food, if Sandra kept such a thing. Each time Kayleigh opened the pantry, she was taken aback. Sandra took organization to a whole new level. Each shelf was labeled and all the boxes sat in descending order by size. All canned food faced out according to size as well.

Despite diving deep into the pantry shelves, no chips magically appeared. No Snickers Bars or Twix lay hidden behind all the healthy choices.

The refrigerator held a plethora of fresh fruit, prepared salads, and meal kits. But nothing remotely resembling comforting junk food.

Kayleigh pulled open the freezer and had an *ah-ha* moment. She'd discovered Sandra's secret. Five tubs of ice cream in various flavors. "Rocky Road and Moose Tracks," she said, grabbing two of the tubs.

She filled a bowl with the combination of both and stowed them back in the freezer with a smile. Carrying the bowl to the back deck, Kayleigh sat on one of the padded loungers in the shade of the overhang.

Knowing her friend Sam would be visiting cheered her immensely. Well, that and the mound of frozen delight now sliding down her throat. Rocky and Luna padded through the open back door, sniffed Kayleigh's outstretched legs, and wandered into the yard.

After a nice long nap, she'd think about what to do about Gary Golden, dream killer and thief.

Holden and Jenna shared a chicken salad sandwich and a bowl of French onion soup. Jenna chatted about her trip to Florida and the cute decorations she'd purchased at the trade show she'd attended.

Holden listened with half an ear. His thoughts kept returning to Kayleigh and her dilemma about the music producer who'd disappeared with her money. It hit too close to home. What that guy had done was like David's theft. Holden tried to think of a way he could use his money to help find the guy.

Injustice brought his anger to a boil. Just like the organization assisting former sex workers in Thailand, Holden was compelled to do something.

"You're not even listening," Jenna said.

Holden sent her a sheepish look. "Sorry."

Jenna smirked. "Were you thinking about your new admin?"

Holden's face grew hot. "Actually, I was. But not in the way you're suggesting."

"Oh, really? Do tell."

Would it be a betrayal for him to talk to Jenna about Kayleigh's problem? "I'll tell you, but you have to promise not to say anything."

Jenna leaned forward and rested her arms on the table. "Sounds intriguing. Sure, I promise."

Holden gave the abbreviated version of what Kayleigh had told him about the music producer and his disappearance.

Jenna's jaw dropped. "That's terrible. What are you planning, dear brother?"

Holden slumped in his chair. "I'm not sure. She may not welcome my interference."

"It wouldn't be interference if you did a little digging. Surely, she isn't the first one this has happened to."

Holden got to his feet. "You're right, as usual, Sis," he said, dropping a kiss on her head. "I'm going to make a phone call."

An hour later, Holden sat back in his comfy desk

chair and smiled. He'd set an investigation in motion. Now to wait and see what his private investigator would turn up.

Downstairs, he found Jenna with her purse slung over one shoulder. "Going out?"

"I'm going to hang out with some friends."

"Have fun."

Jenna batted her eyelashes. "Um, can I borrow your car?"

Holden laughed. "Sure." He shook a finger at her. "But no speeding. I know how you drive."

Jenna smiled. "I can't make any promises." She headed for the door and spoke over her shoulder. "Don't wait up."

Holden experienced a stab of jealousy. Since his cancer diagnosis, he'd sunk further and further into isolation. He didn't want anyone to see him struggling to walk with his cane. Rival companies would love to take advantage of his weakness. Just like his company's board of directors.

If it weren't for Andrew and Jenna, the only interactions he'd have would be his parents and his board. And that was a mixed bag. Some on the board, like Stanley, were still dismayed at his dad's retirement. They didn't think he was capable of taking the reins and running the corporation. They felt his lack of years meant he was too immature.

But Dad's words rang in his brain. A Scripture verse from First Timothy. "Let no one despise your youth."

Sure, Dad. How do I keep men like Stanley from despising me?

Holden glanced up the stairs, trying to decide if he

wanted to return to his office and work, or stay downstairs and take a nap.

The nap won.

Later, after eating a meal left by his housekeeper, Holden headed outside to sit on the back patio. The temperature dropped and a soft breeze blew some of the humidity in the direction of the lake. Maybe tomorrow he'd make the effort to walk down to the dock and see if his kayak was still hanging on its rack.

He sank onto one of the deck chairs and stretched out his bad leg. His attention was pulled to shuffling in the hedge separating his yard from the Donaldson's. Soon two furry beasts charged into his backyard.

Holden frowned as the mutts raced around his yard, sniffing bushes and marking their territory. Kayleigh must have left the gate open. He didn't know whether to be irritated or amused. A few minutes later, Kayleigh's head peeked through the bushes.

"Are Rocky and Luna here?" she asked.

"Unfortunately, yes."

"I'm really sorry. Let me grab them."

Holden wanted to keep her near for a bit longer. "They're fine. Why don't you join me?" He indicated the frosty glass sitting in front of him on the table.

She looked hesitant as she tentatively approached.

"I promise not to bite your head off," Holden said.

He was rewarded with a smile. "Okay." Kayleigh pulled out a chair and sat.

"Would you like some iced tea or lemonade?" Holden asked.

"No, I'm okay." She perched on the edge of the

chair as if ready to spring up any moment.

"I heard you playing your guitar the other night. You have a beautiful voice."

Holden couldn't see her face in the waning daylight. She didn't answer.

"Your voice reminds me of my mother. She used to sing my brother and sister and me to sleep."

Kayleigh sniffled. "That's sweet."

"What about you? What memories do you have from your childhood?"

Chapter 13

Kayleigh scooted back on the chair and regarded Holden through narrowed eyes. Why was he being so nice? She'd gotten used to his grumpiness, and this was a side of him she wasn't sure she wanted to know. It would be too easy to be attracted to Holden. With his wicked good looks, and now, his sweet personality, she'd soon be too far down the rabbit hole to escape.

"My dad was the one who sang to me."

"Is he a musician?" Holden asked.

"He was. I guess he still is. My dad was in a band when he and my mom met." Did Holden really want to hear this?

"Go on."

Kayleigh sucked in a breath. "When my mom got pregnant with me, my dad gave up his dream of being a rock star. He went back to school and got his finance degree. Now he's in a band with some other old guys. They play at nursing homes for a few dollars."

"Does he regret his choice?"

Kayleigh considered Holden's question. "I don't know. I've never asked him about it."

"Do you have siblings?"

"Nope. Just me. Sometimes I envy people with big families."

Holden chuckled. "It isn't all it's cracked up to be. I used to wish I was an only child."

Kayleigh had no idea how to respond to that statement. The silence lengthened between them. But not an awkward silence. With the soft sounds of the lake slapping against the shore in the distance, and the faint breeze rustling the trees, Kayleigh relaxed.

Worries over her financial situation and Gary Golden's disappearance dissipated in the curtain of darkness.

Holden's scent drifted toward her, like eucalyptus and mint. A pleasant smell that reminded Kayleigh of her dad. Kayleigh was beginning to be concerned with how attracted she was to Holden. Sitting here in the semi-darkness, a sense of calm radiated from him to her. As if Holden's guard was dropped, and she was safe from her circumstances.

Holden tapped something on his phone. A moment later, the pool lit with soft light and the sound of the waterfall. The air, still and silent, was thick with unspoken emotion. Kayleigh's throat ached with unshed tears. Sympathy for Holden's illness and recovery, and jealousy over his siblings' love and connection with each other.

Kayleigh cleared her throat and broke the silence. "Where's your sister?"

"She went out with some friends. She'll be home late."

Kayleigh shifted on the padded seat, uncomfortable with the intimacy of sitting with Holden in the semidarkness. Alone.

His next question shocked her. "Will you play something for me?"

"Oh, no. I don't think so." Kayleigh sprang to her feet. "I should go."

Holden put out a hand as if to stop her. "Please don't go. Not yet."

Kayleigh heard the loneliness in his voice. What must it be like, living in this huge mansion alone? She'd felt the same in Sandra and Robert's house. She missed people. As adorable as Rocky and Luna were, they were no substitute for actual humans.

"Please," Holden said. "Won't you get your guitar and play for me?"

She wanted to say no. It was different playing in front of a bar full of half-drunk men. In front of one man? Way too intimate.

Kayleigh chewed her lip, and agreed, against her better judgement. "Give me a moment. Is it okay if the dogs stay here?" The pups lounged on the deck by their feet.

"Sure."

She marched through the opening in the bushes and into the house. Marty still sat on the living room coffee table.

"Well, Marty, it's show time I guess." She pulled the strap over her shoulder and plucked a few strings, making a slight adjustment.

Nerves skittered up her spine at the thought of playing for Holden. What if his nasty personality returned and he laughed at her? Kayleigh bit her lip and considered staying in the house. If it weren't for the dogs, she would have.

With a sigh, she returned to Holden's place, guitar

strapped against her back.

Holden sat in the same spot. He leaned down and stroked on of the pups on the head. Kayleigh couldn't tell them apart in the darkness. Ambient light from the pool reflected on Holden's face, deepening the stubble on his cheeks. Dang, the guy was hot.

Kayleigh sat in the chair she'd vacated and concentrated on strumming a few chords.

"Play a song you've written," Holden said. This time his words sounded sincere rather than demanding.

Kayleigh focused on Marty and said, "This is something I'm working on. Being here, at Sandra and Robert's, surrounded by all this ..." She waved a hand toward Holden's house and the swimming pool. "... reminded me that I'm a pretty simple girl."

When Holden didn't respond, Kayleigh inhaled and began to play.

I ain't no French-tipped champagne kinda girl
Won't take your Tesla Maserati to make my head twirl
Just give me blue jeans, porch swings, bare feet
Give me a song with a good ole country beat

Don't want no 5 star 5 carat up town
Won't wear no high heels high fashion designer gown
Just give me blue jeans, porch swings, bare feet
Give me a song with a good ole country beat

Keep your two dozen two carat high class
Give me moonshine whiskey in a plastic glass
Don't need no Garth Brooks front row Instagram

I'd rather dance in the park with a country band
Walk home in the dark holding hands
Give me blue jeans, porch swings, bare feet
Give me a song with a good ole country beat

Won't eat no food from fancy French menus
You can keep your truffles and your uptown venues
I'll have my crawfish boiled and my corn on the cob
Won't eat no meals with no east coast snobs

Faith, family, friends and the bible
Cross my heart, say a prayer, go to a revival

I've got dirt on my knees and my hands are rough
Daddy says country girls gotta be tough
Life is hard, lovin' is too
Find the one who loves you for you

So give me blue jeans, porch swings, bare feet
Give me a song with a good ole country beat
Hug me hard and kiss me sweet
Pick me up and swing me round
Get me lost in that country sound
 Blue jeans, porch swings, bare feet, and country beat
 Blue jeans, porch swings, bare feet, and country beat

Holden held his breath as the last notes from Kayleigh's guitar faded on the evening breeze. Something went *clunk* in his chest. He closed his eyes against the sudden rush of feelings flooding through his body.

He'd just fallen for this red-haired beauty. That song. Those words. They took him back to his childhood when he and Andrew and Jenna ran barefoot on their parents' property. Before his dad had steered Holden Holdings into a billion-dollar enterprise. When swimming in the lake was the highlight of their day. When riding bikes until dark and rushing into the house, sweaty and hungry, meant peanut butter and jelly sandwiches on white bread.

Kayleigh's voice interrupted his thoughts. "I know it needs some work."

Holden forced his words through his throat, clogged with emotion. "It was perfect."

Kayleigh's head was still bent over her guitar. She flicked a glance up and back down.

"Don't second-guess yourself," Holden said. "That was brilliant."

"Thanks."

The silence lengthened between them. Words Holden wanted to say swirled in his head, but they remained unspoken. He didn't want to scare her away with his sudden realization that he was smitten.

Smitten. Such an old-fashioned word for what churned in his chest. He was falling in love. The thought terrified him. Since his cancer, he'd shut himself off from the opposite sex. How unfair to start a relationship with someone, knowing they'd probably want something he couldn't provide.

Holden shoved his chair back and used his cane to help him stand. "I need to go."

He despised the shakiness in his voice and in his legs. He couldn't make out Kayleigh's expression and for that he was glad.

"Close the gate when you leave."

Holden retreated into his house and slowly made his way upstairs. He undressed and sank into bed, mentally slapping himself on the forehead. Tomorrow, he'd tell Kayleigh he no longer needed her services as his administrative assistant. He'd pay her for two weeks and let her go.

It was better that way. Kayleigh deserved someone who could give her a family.

But her song had struck a chord he couldn't get rid of. Her words echoed in his brain as he fell into a fitful sleep.

Disturbing dreams caused him to wake up every hour. Dreams of falling into his swimming pool and being unable to kick himself to the surface. He woke gasping for breath. At two a.m., Holden gave up the pretense of sleep.

Kayleigh watched Holden stomp into his house. What just happened? She'd played her song, he'd complimented her, and then *poof*—Mr. Cranky Pants returned with a vengeance.

Despite his positive comments, imposter syndrome raised its ugly head. Why did she bother trying to be a musician? Her parents were right. She needed to find a real job, go back to school, and learn how to do something productive.

"Come on, mutts," Kayleigh said to the sleeping pups. She nudged Rocky with her foot. "Time to go home."

They lumbered to their feet and yawned. Kayleigh made sure to close and secure the gate after they'd gone through. Her shoulders slumped as she led the dogs into the house.

She climbed into bed and mentally rehearsed the evening. She thought she and Holden had shared a moment. Apparently, she was wrong. He'd only been nice about her song because he didn't want to hurt her feelings. For once.

Kayleigh turned on her side and plumped the pillow under her head. Tears burned in her eyes and dripped down her cheeks, wetting her pillow.

In the morning, the dark clouds scuttling across the sky added to Kayleigh's mood. Even the dogs seemed depressed. After a quick jaunt outside to do their business, Luna and Rocky settled back on their beds in the kitchen nook.

Her day brightened a smidge with a text from Samantha.

Sam: I'm on my way. Be there in an hour.

Seeing her bestie and crying on Sam's shoulder was just what Kayleigh needed. She sent a quick text to Holden, asking if he needed her today.

While waiting for his answer, Kayleigh wrested with the espresso machine and prepared a strong cup of java. She'd need at least two and maybe three cups after a night of tossing on the too soft bed.

Holden: No

Holden's one-word text brought relief she wouldn't have to face him, and irritation that he couldn't be bothered to use more words.

Stupid jerk. Deliciously handsome, but still a jerk. It would be best if she told Holden she couldn't work for him anymore. It was too easy to be attracted to him. The last thing she needed was a romantic entanglement that couldn't go anywhere. In less than a month, she'd be finished dog-sitting and would move on to ... where?

Her parents would love to have her back home. Mom, in particular, would relish being able to run Kayleigh's life again. If Kayleigh even hinted she might have to move back, Mom would have a college schedule completely mapped out before Kayleigh reached the end of the Donaldson's curving driveway.

How quickly her life had gone from Nashville hopeful to loser.

Steam rose from the wood deck as rain pelted down, creating a fog machine effect. Kayleigh carried her second cup of coffee outside and stood under the overhang. Her phone buzzed in her pocket with an incoming text. She ignored it. It was either Holden, who she didn't want to talk to, or Samantha, updating her on when she'd arrive.

With a sigh, Kayleigh returned to the house. The dogs had been fed, and there was nothing for her to do. Except check the mailbox. A stiff breeze chased the clouds and rain to the west and the sun made its appearance.

After a quick glance at the pups, Kayleigh grabbed the mailbox key hanging on a hook inside the pantry and headed out the front door. The cluster mailbox was up the road, halfway between the Donaldson's and Holden's driveways. It would be just her luck for Holden to check his mail at the same time.

Then she reminded herself he probably had 'people' to take care of such mundane tasks.

In the box, Kayleigh pulled out the Donaldson's mail and carried it back to the house. She tossed it on the kitchen island.

Pulling her phone from her pocket, she saw she'd received two texts.

Samantha: Almost there

Holden: Leaving for Thailand tonight. Don't come the rest of the week.

Kayleigh heaved a sigh of relief. She wouldn't have to face Mr. Cranky Pants while Sam was here.

The doorbell rang, stirring Luna and Rocky to their feet. They rushed to the front door and stood with tails wagging.

Kayleigh threw open the door, grabbed her bestie in a hug, and burst into tears.

Chapter 14

Holden reclined his seat on the Challenger 350 jet and closed his eyes. The seventeen-hour flight would be a chance to get caught up on the sleep he'd lost after hearing Kayleigh sing. Guilt plagued him after his harsh response to her text.

It was better this way. Holden needed to distance himself from her. There was no sense in starting something that couldn't be finished. If he kept telling himself that, maybe he'd believe it.

Holden turned his thoughts to the Thailand school for women. The highlight of his month was his regular trip to check on the progress of the beauty school. The women who'd been rescued from the sex trade learned how to cut hair, apply makeup, and how to do manicures. Holden's money enabled the school to offer room and board while the women attended. They were encouraged but not required to attend weekly church services. Holden also donated generously to the church in Ekkamai.

It warmed his heart to see the women who were once bowed down with shame become confident and assured of their worth in God. He and David had planned to expand the school to include young men and boys who were also trapped in human sexual slavery.

But when Holden was diagnosed with cancer and was in the hospital, David decided that the generous salary he was paid wasn't enough. His embezzlement was more than thievery of money. He'd taken Holden's trust, friendship, and brotherhood and cast it away like it was of no value.

He wouldn't do the same to Kayleigh by letting her think there was a possibility of a relationship with him.

That thought carried him into a restless sleep.

He woke to the flight attendant touching him on the shoulder.

"We will be descending in about sixty minutes," she said, handing him a frosty glass of orange juice. "Would you like to freshen up before I bring your meal?"

Holden rubbed his face. "Yes, please."

The attendant returned to the galley. Holden downed the juice and used his cane to help him stand. He bent from one side to the other to loosen his stiff muscles from sitting so long.

Holden used the bathroom to shave and splash water over his face and head. Once they landed in Bangkok, he'd catch a ride to the hotel and shower before heading to the school.

He picked at the continental breakfast the flight attendant set before him. Half a croissant, a few strawberries, a bit of yogurt, and he was full. Lack of activity had made him weak. Another frustration.

The jet barely bumped as it hit the landing strip at Bangkok Suvarnabhumi Airport. Holden deplaned and headed to Customs. This is where he needed Donna. His assistant made the monthly trip with him and made sure they cleared customs. Her knowledge of Thai was invaluable. Without her, Holden was forced to make himself understood to the customs agents.

By the time he reached the hotel, his head ached, and his hip felt like he was being stabbed with a knife. At almost a thousand dollars a night, Capella Bangkok Resort offered the comfort and privacy Holden was used to. The fabulous views of the City were an added bonus.

Holden showered and donned a pair of tan slacks and a moisture-wicking golf shirt. With daily temperatures in the nineties, he'd be sweating during the non-air-conditioned taxi ride to the suburb of Ekkamai.

Holden downed some ibuprofen and headed to the lobby.

"May I call a cab for you, sir?" the man at the front desk asked.

"Yes, please."

"For just you? Or will someone be joining you?"

"No. Just me."

"May I find a companion for you?"

Holden stiffened. He searched the clerk's face for any expression of lasciviousness and found none. But Holden knew what he was asking. This city offered a plethora of 'companions' ranging from children to those who preferred the same sex.

This was another disadvantage of traveling without Donna.

"That won't be necessary," Holden said, turning to walk toward the front door.

The taxi took him from the bustling city of Bangkok to the quieter Ekkamai suburb. He climbed out of the taxi and stood on the sidewalk staring at the nondescript building that housed the school. No sign or indication that a bustling school existed behind the closed door and shuttered windows. Many of the women feared retaliation for leaving the men who 'managed' their lives.

He knocked on the door and it was immediately opened by an older Thai woman who wrapped him in a warm hug.

"Mr. Holden, welcome," she exclaimed, releasing him.

"It's been a while, hasn't it, Anong," Holden said, closing the door behind him and locking it. His last visit had been a few days before the test results came in with the devastating cancer diagnosis. It was now twelve weeks past his surgery to remove the tumor.

"Come in, come in," Anong said. Her face beamed with a huge smile. "We have been praying for you, Mr. Holden." Anong's face fell. "We were so worried when we heard the news."

Holden sent her a closed-mouth smile. "Prayers are always welcome." He shifted his weight from his bad leg.

"Let's go to the classroom." Anong led Holden down a dark hallway, then another, and finally into a brightly lit room resembling a beauty salon.

He sat in one of the shampoo bowl chairs and watched the activity with a smile of satisfaction. Some of the young women covered their mouths as they giggled to see a man in their domain. Others kept their distance, no doubt still uncomfortable around the opposite sex.

Anong sat in the chair next to him and watched as

the instructor spoke. "Remember when Mali was rescued?" Anong asked, inclining her head to the woman now teaching.

Holden remembered well the scared girl with two swollen eyes and a broken rib. Mali had refused to speak for weeks. Her bruises and bones healed more quickly than the psychological damage caused by her pimp.

"I remember," Holden said. "It is truly a miracle to see her today."

Anong crossed herself and clasped her hands together in a prayerful gesture. "Amen. If not for you, she would most likely be dead."

"Not me," Holden protested. "It was the Lord. I just facilitated her healing."

This was what Holden lived for. Miraculous transformation and spiritual healing.

Kayleigh settled Samantha into one of the spare upstairs bedrooms and returned to the living room to wait.

Samantha swept down the stairs in a cloud of expensive-smelling perfume. Kayleigh smothered a flare of envy at Sam's look of effortless chic. Her super-model friend wore a pair of pale pink linen capris and a flowered top. Kayleigh guessed Sam's outfit cost more than Kayleigh made in a week at the Donaldson's.

Sam plopped onto the sofa and tucked one leg under her. "What's going on, Kay? Why the tears?"

Kayleigh sucked in a breath and blew it out. "I don't even know where to begin."

"Start with Mr. Cranky Pants," Sam said with a

grin.

"How 'bout I don't."

"There's a story there, and I can't wait to hear it."

"Let me start with Gary Golden," Kayleigh said. She repeated the sad story about paying the guy a pile of money and his subsequent disappearance.

"Sweetie, that is one of the saddest things I've heard lately." Sam shifted on the sofa. "Can I help? You know I'd give you the money in a heartbeat."

Kayleigh sighed. "I know you would. But I can't. I have to do this on my own." Sam had made a ton of money modeling since she was fourteen. But since her marriage to billionaire Logan Walters, Kayleigh's financial loss would be less than Sam and Logan's monthly discretionary spending.

"What *are* you going to do?" Sam asked.

"I'm going to give up songwriting and singing." There. She'd said it out loud. It hurt to hear the words go out of her mouth.

"You can't do that," Sam exclaimed. "You're too good. You have a gift."

But Kayleigh was shaking her head before Sam finished speaking. "I'm not. I played my latest song for, you know," she tilted her head toward next door.

"Holden Jeffries? What did he say?"

Kayleigh's cheeks burned. "First, he said it was brilliant. Then, he pretty much ordered me to go home." Kayleigh squirmed with remembered embarrassment.

"He didn't." Sam was suitably outraged as a best friend should be. "What exactly did he say? I want every word. Every detail."

"He said it was perfect. And brilliant. Then he stood and told me to close the gate behind me. I honestly thought we'd shared a moment."

Sam slouched back against the sofa cushions. "Hmm."

"What does 'hmm' mean?"

Sam's face broke into a wide smile. "I think you like him." Sam's voice took on a sing-song quality as she quoted some lines from *Miss Congeniality*. "You think he's gorgeous. You want to kiss him."

Kayleigh laughed despite herself. "Stop."

Sam raised her hands in surrender. "You're crushing on him."

Kayleigh slapped her forehead. "Ugh. You're right." What was she going to do about it?

JANE DALY

Chapter 15

Holden ended his visit with a dinner with Pastor Bho at the resort where Holden was staying.

"I cannot thank you enough for all you have done for our community," Pastor Bho said.

Holden waved off his compliment. "I am happy to do it. You're the one who is doing all the work, Pastor."

Under Bho's leadership and care, the church had embraced the women society turned their back on because of their former occupation.

Holden sipped his after-dinner cappuccino. "I'd like you to find another building for sale to start a similar school for boys and young men."

Pastor Bho's face lit up. "I know just the place. I will make some inquiries and have something ready for your next trip." The pastor's face clouded. "How is your health, my brother? Will you continue your monthly visits?"

Holden rubbed his hip and frowned. "I am having some scans next month. I would appreciate your prayers that the scans show no cancer."

"I will do that. May I also ask our leadership team to pray?"

"Of course." Holden drained the last of his coffee

and rubbed his weary face. "I should get to bed. But I want you to think about what classes we should offer when the school for boys opens."

"Of course, Mr. Holden. I will work with our team and present some options for you next month."

Holden struggled to his feet. "I have arranged a car to take you back to Ekkamai. It should be waiting out front."

Pastor Bho stood and bowed slightly. "A million thanks, my friend."

They shook hands and Pastor Bho pulled Holden into an embrace. "I will pray for you, my brother."

Holden returned to his suite and stood at the window looking at the lights of Bangkok. Who would think such a beautiful city could hide such a dark underbelly. Human trafficking of every sort could be found in the dank alleys and cheap hotels.

If his former friend, David hadn't stolen several million dollars, the school for boys would have already been started. Holden's grip tightened on his cane. What was taking so long for the courts to set a date for David's trial?

His phone buzzed with an incoming email. Holden sat on a bench at the end of the king-size bed and opened it. His private investigator had sent a link.

"I might have found your friend's Golden boy. Check out the link. It's a police report. The guy was picked up for speeding and a bunch of other stuff came up."

Holden opened the link and tried to read the small print on his phone. His eyes burned with fatigue. He'd look at it later on his laptop. Right now, the bed shouted his name. He stripped off his clothes and crawled between the sheets.

He woke several hours later with a pounding headache and covered in sweat. He limped to the bathroom and downed some ibuprofen and a bottle of water. He better not be getting sick.

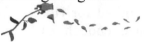

Kayleigh took Samantha and the dogs to the shore of Seneca Lake. The day was sunny and hot, and the women took of their shoes and waded in the cool water.

"It's beautiful here," Sam said, gazing at the green hills across the lake.

"Yes, it is. But not as pretty as your place on Lake Skaneateles."

"Oh, I don't know. I think all the Finger Lakes have their own beauty."

They sat on the shore and watched Rocky and Luna frolic in the water.

"When does your crush come back from his trip?" Sam asked.

Kayleigh sent her friend a death glare. "Stop saying that."

Sam's face was full of innocence. "Saying what?"

Kayleigh snorted. "Fine. So, I have a little crush on Mr. Cranky Pants." She used her index finger to begin a count. "One, I doubt he feels the same. Two, I work for him, remember? How awkward to date your boss. Three, I'm leaving in a few weeks. And four . . ." Her voice trailed off. "There is no four."

"So, you have several weeks to find out if Holden feels the same. All that other stuff is just noise."

"But I still work for him."

Sam shrugged. "So quit."

"I need the money." Kayleigh calculated how much she'd earn from the Donaldson's. It would be enough to pay her bills for a couple of months until she figured out what she was going to do. Her stomach felt like it did a curlicue at the thought of moving back in with her parents. If she worked for Holden for the entire time, she'd maybe have enough cash to find a place by herself.

Probably not in Nashville, though. Rents there were ridiculous. She'd have to find a roommate. However, if she did give up her dream of being a singer songwriter, she wouldn't have to move to Nashville.

Sam nudged Kayleigh's shoulder with hers. "What are you thinking about?"

"Trying to untangle the wad of thoughts in my brain."

"Try praying about it. Works for me."

Kayleigh pulled in a breath and blew it out. "You're right. I've been pretty lax in that area." Which brought her Granny to mind. Since Kayleigh could talk, Granny told her the importance of praying about everything.

Speaking of her grandma, Mom had said she was mailing something from Granny. The mail still sat in a disorganized pile on the kitchen island.

"Let's walk a bit," Sam suggested. She stood and held out a hand to drag Kayleigh to her feet.

Kayleigh called to the dogs. They raced to where she stood and gazed at her in anticipation. "Come on, guys, let's walk."

"They're so well behaved," Sam commented. "While we walk, tell me more about Mr. Cranky."

Something bloomed in Kayleigh's chest as she considered the man. Kayleigh linked her arm with

Sam's as they set out along the shoreline.

"Did you know he's a twin? Well, actually a triplet." Kayleigh's face warmed as she remembered how she thought Jenna was Holden's girlfriend. "He has an identical twin brother and a sister. They were all born at the same time."

"What are the odds of that?"

"I know, right? He's also on the board or involved somehow in this rescue thing in Thailand. They get girls off the street and teach them to cut hair."

"That's awesome," Sam said. "He sounds like a great guy."

Kayleigh considered her answer. "Yeah, except for that whole grumpy thing."

"What was the deal with the health scare? I remember seeing a tiny blurb about it."

"Cancer."

"Yikes. Maybe that's why he's cranky?" Sam pulled on Kayleigh's arm, causing her to stumble. "Maybe cut him some slack. Imagine getting cancer at such a young age."

"Fine. I'll cut him some slack. But I'm still not going to jump into a relationship."

Sam grinned. "So you say. Look what happened to me. I was hiding out from that stalker and met my soulmate, right next door."

"I'm going back to the house. You can stay here and fantasize about my nonexistent love life."

Kayleigh disentangled her arm from her friend and dashed back toward the Donaldson's. She heard Sam's laughter on the breeze blowing from the lake toward the shore.

JANE DALY

Chapter 16

By the time the car service dropped Holden at the airport, his throat was on fire and pressure had built in his chest. Staying in bed would be his best option, but Holden wanted to be home. He wanted his own doctor to see him and to climb into his own bed.

He slept most of the long flight to La Guardia. And on the ride from the airport to his home on Seneca Lake. He dragged himself up the stairs, stripped off his clothes, and fell into bed.

Fueled by fever, Holden dreamed he was baking in the hot sun, adrift on a raft. He woke to rising nausea and barely made it to the bathroom before emptying his stomach.

He squinted against the sunlight pouring through the bathroom window. Conga drums hammered against his skull. The tile was cool under his cheek as he lay panting on the bathroom floor.

After rinsing his mouth, Holden limped back to bed. His phone pinged with a text.

Kayleigh: Do you need me today?

Before responding, Holden sent a group text to his family asking for prayers. Then a text to his on-call physician, asking him to come to the house. His response was immediate.

Doc: I'll be there in an hour and a half.

Holden stayed upright long enough to respond to Kayleigh.

Holden: Come over and let my doctor in.

After reading the text, he added, *Please*.

Holden sank against the pillows. How pathetic was his life that he had to have his assistant—temporary assistant—help him. He'd isolated himself from everyone so no one would see his weakness.

Nice job, loser.

He should have downed some ibuprofen when he was in the bathroom. The thought of getting out of bed again was overwhelming. He fell into a restless sleep. This time, he dreamed Kayleigh was calling him from the end of a long, dark hallway. The walls moved closer and closer together until Holden could barely stand sideways.

"Holden? Holden."

He woke with a start. Kayleigh's voice was real.

"In here." His tongue was thick, and his throat burned when he spoke.

"What in the world?" Kayleigh exclaimed. She laid a cool hand on his hot forehead. "You're burning up."

He was hallucinating. There was no way Kayleigh could actually be in his bedroom.

Several minutes—or maybe an hour—later, she reappeared at his bedside.

"I brought you some ice water and some medicine."

Even his eyes hurt to open them. Through the slits, he spied Kayleigh shoving a plastic cup in his direction.

"Sit up a little and drink."

Holden pushed himself up on his elbows. Kayleigh

held the cup to his lips. Holden managed to get a couple of swallows down.

"Do you have a thermometer?" Kayleigh asked.

"I don't know." His voice came out as a croak.

He closed his eyes and willed his stomach to accept the pills he'd downed. The faint scent of Kayleigh's hair wafted over him as she leaned down again to feel his forehead. If getting sick meant having the soft touch of her hand, Holden would gladly suffer through this.

Kayleigh sent a text to Samantha, who'd been chatting with her husband when Kayleigh left.

Kayleigh: Holden is sick. I'll be here for a while.

She got a thumbs up from Sam.

Holden's doorbell rang, and she dashed down the stairs to the front door. A man stood on the doorstep wearing khaki shorts and a button up cotton shirt.

"Hello," he said. "I'm Doctor Sanford. My last appointment didn't last as long as I expected."

Kayleigh moved aside to let him in. "You do house calls?"

The doctor laughed. "I'm paid very well to do house calls. What's going on with Holden?"

Kayleigh wrung her hands. "He's burning up, and I think he threw up before I got here."

"Has he eaten anything that might have caused it?"

They ascended the stairs. Doctor Sanford shifted his black bag to the other hand and grasped the ornate banister.

"I have no idea. He sent me a text asking me to let you in."

The doctor stopped on the last step. "And you are?"

"I'm Kayleigh. His assistant."

"What happened to Donna?"

"She's on pregnancy leave."

"Ah. Do you know if Holden has traveled lately?"

Kayleigh bit her lip. "He told me he was going to Thailand on business."

"Good to know." Dr. Sanford strode to Holden's bedroom as if he'd been there before.

Which Kayleigh assumed was the case, given Holden's recent surgery. She followed the doctor into Holden's bedroom.

Dr. Sanford set his bag on a chair near the bed. "I'm going to have to ask you to wait outside due to privacy issues."

Kayleigh turned to go, but Holden's strained whisper stopped her.

"She can stay."

The doctor's gaze shifted from Holden to Kayleigh and back to Holden. "If you say so."

He pulled an instrument from his bag and ran it over Holden's forehead. When it beeped, he studied the result.

"You have a fever of 101.5." He grasped Holden's wrist to gauge his pulse. He noted the results on an iPad. "I'm going to listen to your heart."

Kayleigh held her breath, torn between hope and fear, as she listened to Holden's labored breathing. She watched his chest rise and fall as Dr. Sanford carefully moved the stethoscope across Holden's motionless body. Tears blurred her vision, and anxiety twisted inside her, grappling with the possibility that his cancer might have returned. But part of her resisted this thought, clinging to a fragile hope that everything would be all right.

The doctor unwound the stethoscope from his neck and shoved it into his bag. "You have a virus, Holden. I'm going to prescribe some antibiotics just in case. But rest and plenty of fluids and you should feel better in a day or two."

Holden grunted a response.

"I'll check back later today and again tomorrow." He motioned for Kayleigh to follow him out of Holden's bedroom. She took one last look at Holden's prone form before trailing behind the doctor.

When they reached the bottom of the stairs, Kayleigh asked, "Would you like a cup of coffee before you go?"

"Thank you. That would be great."

They stepped into the kitchen and Kayleigh eyed Holden's fancy coffee machine. "I'm not sure how to work this thing."

Dr. Sanford laughed. "How about a bottle of water instead?"

Kayleigh opened the refrigerator with a feeling of unease. She expected Holden to appear at any moment and demand why she was intruding in his personal space.

The doctor set his bag on the floor and reached for the water. He took a long swig.

"I'll call in the prescription and have it delivered here by midafternoon. Will you be here to receive it?"

"I can be," Kayleigh responded. "How do you do that? I mean, order a prescription and have it delivered? I didn't think insurance paid for stuff like that."

Dr. Sanford chuckled. "Holden doesn't have insurance. He pays me to provide boutique medical services, which I do for him and several others. I can get things done expeditiously without having to deal with insurance."

"Seriously? How much does something like that cost?"

Dr. Sanford pursed his lips. "You really don't want to know."

And she didn't. Whatever the cost, it was way above what she currently made. "Well, I'm glad you were here."

The doctor used his water bottle to give her a mock salute. "That's why they pay me the big bucks." He picked up his black bag. "I'll check on Holden later. In the meantime, there's a golf course calling my name."

Kayleigh watched Dr. Sanford see himself out. She pulled her phone from her pocket and called Samantha.

"Is Mr. Cranky Pants working your fingers to the bone?" Sam asked.

"No. He's sick. Like really sick. His doctor just left. And get this. The doctor is on call, like all the time. He's having antibiotics delivered to the house."

"A lot of people use a boutique doctor or medical practice. You pay a certain amount of money every year to have a doctor on call. It beats having to go to urgent care or wait in a germ-filled waiting room."

"Sounds ridiculously bougie."

Sam laughed. "It definitely is."

"How are the dogs?"

"They're fine. I let them out earlier, and now, they're sleeping."

"Do you mind watching them for a while longer? I need to wait here for the prescription delivery."

"I don't mind a bit. I'm reading a good book."

"I can't thank you enough."

"Don't even worry about it. Take care of your boyfriend."

Sam disconnected before Kayleigh could respond. She shook her head and returned upstairs to check on Holden.

JANE DALY

Chapter 17

Holden vaguely remembered being examined by his doctor. Had he imagined Kayleigh touching his head and bringing him a glass of water? He shifted on the bed, trying to find a position to ease the ache in his hip.

His eyes cracked open and focused on the glass of water on the end table. Struggling to a sitting position, he grabbed the glass and chugged it down.

"Want more?"

The voice startled him, and he fumbled with the now empty glass. "Sure." His voice came out as a croak. "My throat feels like I swallowed a pair of scissors."

Kayleigh approached the bed and took the glass from his sweaty hand. "I'll make sure it's nice and icy."

"I take that back," Holden said. "My throat feels like I swallowed glass fragments."

Kayleigh stared at him with a frown. "I'm going to get you some 7-Up. It's my go-to when I'm sick."

Holden flopped back against his pillow. "Whatever." He closed his eyes and was torn between wanting her to leave and desiring her to stay.

Kayleigh stomped down the stairs in a huff. Holden's off-hand 'whatever' remark irritated her more than she wanted to admit. If she weren't a nice person, she'd leave Mr. Cranky to suffer alone.

But she couldn't in good conscience do that. Instead, she used Sandra's food ordering app. She'd make Holden some of her granny's chicken and dumplings. Like chicken soup, but better. That man lying upstairs needed some meat on his bones.

She knew Granny's recipe by heart. She placed the food order and scheduled it for delivery to Holden's house. While she waited, she'd call Granny.

Granny answered on the first ring. "I was wonderin' when you were gonna call me, child. Did you get my letter?"

"Oh, Granny, I'm sorry. I'm the worst granddaughter ever."

"Don't you worry your pretty little head. I sent you a little somethin' I picked up when your mama and I were in New York."

"What is it?" Kayleigh remembered setting the Donaldson's mail on the kitchen island, but she hadn't bothered to go through the envelopes.

"It wouldn't be a surprise if I told you, now would it?"

Kayleigh chuckled. "I guess not. I'll check when I get back to the Donaldson's."

"Where are you now?" Granny asked.

Kayleigh bit her lip as she contemplated her answer. Granny wasn't as nosy as Mom, but she still wanted lots of details on Kayleigh's life.

"I'm doing a little admin work for the next-door neighbor."

"Is he single? Good-looking? Available?"

Kayleigh laughed. "Granny, you're too much. Yes, he's single. Yes, he's good-looking. I don't know if he's available." Emotionally available, doubtful. Holden could use a personality transplant.

"You better find out, missy. I can hear your biological clock ticking. Tick tock."

"I'm only twenty-four, ma'am. Hardly beyond my prime."

Granny clicked her tongue. "Don't wait too long."

"I won't." The doorbell rang. "Gotta go, Granny. My food delivery is here. I'm making your famous chicken and dumplings."

"I love, you, Kayleigh."

"Love you too, Gran."

Kayleigh disconnected and opened the door to find a bag of groceries on the porch. The red taillights of a compact car slowed to take the final turn of Holden's driveway.

She carried the food into the house and unpacked the items, placing them on the counter. She filled a plastic cup with ice and poured 7-Up over the ice. Kayleigh tapped her foot while she waited for the foam to settle.

She carried the cup up the stairs and braced herself. "Time to face the monster."

Holden lay with one arm slung over his forehead. Kayleigh took a moment to admire his sleeping form. Dang, the man was hot, despite being ill.

She tiptoed to his bedside and touched his cheek. Yup, still burning up.

Holden cracked his eyes open and stared up with glassy eyes. "What?"

Kayleigh held the cup out. "I brought you some 7-Up. It'll help keep you hydrated."

Holden pushed himself up on his elbows and took the cup. Their fingers brushed. His fingers felt hot.

"How are you feeling?" Kayleigh asked.

Holden swallowed some of the cold liquid and grunted. "Like I want to die."

"Dr. Sanford said he was having some antibiotics delivered. Can I get you anything?"

"How 'bout some Tylenol or something. In my bathroom." Holden shoved the cup in Kayleigh's direction and sank back against his pillow.

Kayleigh set the cup on the nightstand and walked into Holden's attached bathroom, which was bigger than her room back in Nashville. She stood in the doorway, uncomfortable with the feeling of intimacy being in his bathroom.

A toothbrush lay on the counter, along with an electric razor and a hand razor. Next to the sink sat a wadded-up towel. Kayleigh eased open the medicine chest, trying not to poke through the various bottles of aftershave and hair gel. She found the ibuprofen and read the instructions. Shaking two into her palm, she carried them back into Holden's bedroom.

"Here you go," Kayleigh said, bumping the edge of his bed with one hip.

Holden held out his hand, and she dropped the pills into his palm.

"This isn't Tylenol," he said, squinting at the capsules.

"I didn't see Tylenol. This will work just as well."

He popped them into his mouth and reached for the 7-Up.

Kayleigh waited for 'thank you.' She might as well ask for a miracle. There was no 'thanks' coming her way. She mentally chastised Holden's parents for not teaching him basic manners.

Speaking of parents, wouldn't Holden's folks want to know he was sick?

"Do you want me to let your folks know you aren't feeling well?"

"No. They worry too much as it is. I think I sent them a text."

Kayleigh winced. His words sounded like they were forced through a sieve. "Okay, then. I'm going back downstairs. I'm making some chicken and dumplings."

Holden's teeth chattered in the growing silence. "I'm freezing."

Kayleigh pulled his covers up to his chin. "You'll feel better once the ibuprofen kicks in."

She ran downstairs to put the whole chicken in a pot and set it to boil. Once it was simmering, she'd go back upstairs and check on her patient.

JANE DALY

Chapter 18

Holden couldn't remember when he'd felt more miserable. Chemo hadn't been a picnic, but it didn't make him feel like he was burning up one minute and chilled to the bone the next.

He fell into an uneasy sleep and dreamed crazy dreams. In the first one, he and Kayleigh rode in a speedboat. He made a sharp turn and Kayleigh plunged into an angry, churning ocean. He dove in to save her, but she sank just out of his reach. He woke, gasping for breath.

Turning onto his good side, Holden slept, again dreaming of Kayleigh. In this dream, she was kissing him, her lips hot on his. He tried to tell her he couldn't promise her a future, but he couldn't get the words out.

When he woke, his pillow was damp with sweat. He pushed himself up and drank the rest of the 7-Up, wincing against the daggers stabbing in his throat.

He had to pee. Holden swung his legs over the side of the bed and braced himself against the swoop of vertigo. He stood, grasping for his cane.

"What do you think you're doing?"

The angry female voice belonged to Kayleigh.

"I have to pee." He squinted at her through scratchy

eyes.

"Let me help." Kayleigh rushed to his side and grabbed his arm.

"Are you planning to hold my hand during the entire process?"

Holden enjoyed the red spots appearing on her cheeks, despite his discomfort. Talking stung like he'd swallowed fire.

"I'll help you to the door, and you can do the rest on your own."

Holden loved her spunkiness. His thoughts shifted to his dream. He sneaked a look at her lips. They were pressed together, probably in annoyance.

Holden did his business, washed his hands, and splashed water over his face. The mirror revealed his unshaven cheeks and dark circles under his eyes. He limped back to bed to find Kayleigh had exchanged his sweaty pillow for the one on the other side of the bed.

"How are you feeling?" Kayleigh asked, "Any better?"

"A little," he admitted. "I'll be glad when the fever breaks."

"That will be great. You'll feel better once it does. You'll probably want to take a shower too."

Holden fell back against the pillow and regarded her through half-closed eyelids. "Are you offering to help me?"

Kayleigh glared. "I'm going to chalk that comment up to your fever."

Holden chuckled and grimaced. "Got any more of that bubbly stuff?"

Kayleigh looked like she wanted to tell him off.

"Please?"

She breathed in and huffed the breath out through her nose. "Fine." She shook a finger at him. "But not more suggestive comments." She flounced out of his bedroom.

Holden smiled. He was falling for this woman. Nope, that ship had sailed. He'd fallen like a brick tossed from a third-story window. Then he frowned, remembering his disability. A woman like Kayleigh would want the whole package—a man who could give her children. A man without a death sentence hanging over his head. All the specialists said if his scans stayed clear for five years, he could look forward to a long life. In the meantime, five years was a long time to wait for a clean bill of health.

And a long time to ask a woman to wait.

Kayleigh checked the chicken she'd stripped off the carcass. The stew was coming to a nice rolling boil. She'd be able to drop in the dumplings she'd rolled out on the cutting board she'd found. She took a spoonful of the broth, blew on it until it was cool, and tasted.

"Perfect," she said. Kayleigh sent a quick text to Samantha.

Kayleigh: I'm making some of Granny's chix and dumps

Sam: Save me some. I love Granny's Southern cooking.

Kayleigh sent her a thumbs up. Can you watch the dogs for a bit longer?

Sam: Absolutely. I am being super lazy and loving it

Kayleigh set the phone on the counter, turned the

heat down on the chicken, and filled Holden's cup with ice and 7-Up.

She carried it up the massive staircase, pausing to stare down into the living room. Maybe when she became a famous songwriter, she could afford to live somewhere where she wasn't constantly bumping into walls, furniture, or other people.

Reality smacked her in the face when she remembered her current predicament. No job waiting after this dog sitting gig, her savings account drained after Golden's theft, and now suffering from song writer's block.

Not to mention the incredibly good-looking guy upstairs who she was currently nursing back to health. Kayleigh alternated between wanting to stroke his cheek and smother him with a pillow.

Holden was asleep when she padded into his bedroom. His phone lit up with a text. Kayleigh picked it up and read what was revealed on the Lock Screen. Something about the proposal his dad had sent. While she studied his phone, it lit up again. A text from Holden's mom:

Mom: Did you make it home from Thailand? Are you okay? Got your family text asking for prayer.

The doorbell rang, a musical chime that split the silence. Kayleigh bounded back down the stairs. At this rate, she'd lose ten pounds just going from Holden's kitchen to his bedroom.

Dr. Sanford stood on the porch holding a white bag. Kayleigh threw open the door.

"Is that what I think it is?" she asked.

"I thought I'd bring the prescription by myself and check on our patient."

Kayleigh chewed on the word 'our.' Did Dr. Sanford think she lived here? That Holden and she were …

The doctor's face held no suggestion that there was more going on than boss and employee.

"I think his fever has gone down. But it hasn't broken. He's been drinking 7-Up."

Dr. Sanford smiled. "Oh, the old 7-Up remedy. Takes me back to my childhood."

"Me too. Granny always brought me 7-Up and soda crackers when I was sick."

Dr. Sanford waved the white bag. "I'll take this upstairs and check on Holden."

Kayleigh took the opportunity to bring her chicken broth to a boil. She dropped the flat dumplings into the pot one at a time. When they were all in, she used the back of a large soup spoon to gently stir the dumplings. She remembered Granny teaching her to make this dish. Granny always fussed over the nerve of people thinking dumplings were like biscuits that should go on *top* of the soup, not *in* it.

"That smells heavenly," Dr. Sanford said, entering the kitchen.

Kayleigh wiped her flushed cheeks with a towel. "I'd offer you some, but the dumplings have to cure for a bit."

"Oh, that's okay. My wife will have some healthy meal prepared for me when I get home. Probably rabbit food."

Kayleigh laughed at his grim expression.

She leaned back against the counter. "Doc, can I ask you a question?"

Sanford's eyes crinkled when he smiled. "Got a

mole you need me to look at? An undiagnosed illness?"

"Not at all. I want to know about Holden's cancer." She crossed her arms against her stomach. "I know you have HIPPA regulations, but I was alarmed over what I read on the internet."

"Because of his family name, Holden's diagnosis was hardly private. He had a tumor removed from his hip. Synovial sarcoma. A surgeon removed the tumor and followed up with chemo and radiation."

Kayleigh frowned. "Is this virus connected to his cancer?" She held her breath, waiting for Dr. Sanford's answer.

"Not at all. I will say, though, that because of the treatments Holden received, his immune system is compromised. I encouraged him to let his monthly trips to Thailand go until he's built his immunity back up." Dr. Sanford shrugged. "You may have noticed Holden is a stubborn man."

Kayleigh huffed out a humorless laugh. "I've noticed."

Dr. Sanford pulled a business card from his shirt pocket. "Call me anytime if Holden's condition worsened. My biggest concern now is his lungs. Let me know if he has trouble breathing."

Kayleigh took the card and stared at it, a dozen questions tangling up in her brain.

"Do you think I should contact his parents?" Kayleigh asked.

"I'll do it. I'm their doctor, too."

"Thank you," Kayleigh breathed out her relief. She couldn't imagine being sick in bed and not letting her parents know.

Chapter 19

Someone laid a hand on Holden's forehead. He cracked open his eyes, hoping to see Kayleigh. Instead, Dr. Sanford's face filled his vision.

"I brought your prescription," the doctor said. He shook a pill from the bottle and set it on the nightstand. "Take one every twelve hours."

Holden pushed himself up on his elbows. "Thanks, Doc." He took the pill and washed it down with ice-cold 7-Up. The bubbles soothed his throat. How had he never tried the soda before?

"Let me listen to your breathing," Dr. Sanford said, pulling his stethoscope from his bag.

The scope was cold against Holden's back, not an uncomfortable feeling. His face burned from the relentless fever.

"Your lungs sound a little crackly," the doctor said.

"Is that an official diagnosis? Crackly?"

Dr. Sanford's smile was grim. "I'm concerned about pneumonia. Have your girlfriend call or text me if you start to have trouble breathing.

"Girlfriend?"

Dr. Sanford flipped a hand toward the open bedroom door. "The young woman currently in your kitchen making chicken soup."

Holden sank back against the pillow. Exhaustion overtook him. He was too tired to correct his doctor. Kayleigh was not and never would be his girlfriend. Unfortunately.

With his eyes closed, Holden heard Dr. Sanford drop the stethoscope into his black bag.

"I'll check back later tonight," he said.

Holden grunted a reply.

Sometime later, Holden's eyes fluttered open to find Kayleigh standing beside his bed, staring down at him. She'd flipped the light on in his bathroom. Her red hair glowed in the soft light.

"You're awake," she said. "I brought some more ibuprofen. Think you can sit up?"

Holden pulled himself to a sitting position. He held out his hand and Kayleigh dropped two tablets into his palm. The 7-Up had become warm and watery, but it still felt good sliding down his raw throat.

"I made some chicken and dumplings. Want to try a tiny bit?"

Holden shook his head. "Not yet," he croaked.

Kayleigh held his gaze. "Okay. Maybe when the antibiotics kick in."

Holden eased himself back on the pillow. He closed his eyes as weariness overtook him. Kayleigh leaned down and laid a cool hand on his forehead. His breath whooshed from his lungs at her touch. He sucked in a breath.

The smell of chicken soup filled the room, mingling with the scent of Kayleigh's perfume or shampoo. He couldn't tell which.

"Smells good," Holden said.

"That's my granny's famous chicken and dumplings."

"Smells like ..." his words became a jumble in Holden's brain. "I'm uncomfortably attracted to you."

Did he actually say that, or was it only in his mind?

Kayleigh placed her hands on her hips and stared down at Holden's prone form.

'Uncomfortably attracted?' What in the world? Must be the fever talking. The man was gorgeous despite the uneven stubble covering his flushed cheeks. A little mischievousness nudged her to take advantage of his weakness.

"What do you mean, uncomfortably attracted?"

Holden didn't answer for several beats. His voice was a breathy whisper when he responded. "I can't give you children."

Kayleigh smothered a grin. "That's good, since we aren't sleeping together."

Holden waved a hand, eyes closed. "I can't, can't, you know."

Kayleigh frowned. Was he ... impotent? Because of the cancer? No wonder Holden was so grumpy. "I'm sorry." She laid a hand on his shoulder.

Holden grabbed her wrist with a surprisingly strong grip. "No, I'm sorry. You deserve someone who ..." his voice trailed off.

Guilt stabbed Kayleigh's chest. This was wrong on so many levels. She tried to extricate herself from his death-like hold on her wrist.

"Don't go," Holden croaked. He licked dry lips. "You remind me of ... I can't remember." His brow furrowed. "I'm cold." His teeth chattered.

"Let me get another blanket," Kayleigh pulled from his grasp. A search down the hall revealed a linen closet stuffed with extra blankets and sheets. She pulled out a brown blanket and hurried back to Holden's bedroom.

She reached his side and spread the blanket over him, tucking it tight around his body.

"Too hot," he said, pushed against the covers.

Kayleigh chewed her lip as she decided what to do, praying Holden's fever would break soon.

She ran downstairs and turned off the burner under the dumplings. She sent a text to Sam.

Kayleigh: Are you okay alone there? I'm going to spend the night keeping an eye on H

Sam: No problem. Dogs are fine and fed. Take care of your patient.

This was followed by a smiley face, a heart, and the smiley face with heart eyes.

Kayleigh rolled her eyes and headed back to Holden's bedroom. She sat in a wing chair near the bed and stretched her legs out onto an ottoman. Holden's breath was shallow, and he coughed every so often. She said a prayer for his recovery.

Sometime later, she was startled out of sleep by the sound of Holden coughing. She cracked open her eyes and noticed Holden sitting on the edge of his bed.

She sprang to her feet. "How are you? Feeling better?"

"Fever broke," he said in between coughs. "Need a shower."

Kayleigh reached out a hand to steady him as he struggled to his feet. "Let me help you."

They made their way to the bathroom. Kayleigh

released her hold on his arm. "Will you be okay?" She asked.

Holden braced his arms on the counter. "Are you offering to watch in case I fall?"

Kayleigh glared at him. "I told you, no more suggestive comments."

He shifted his gaze to hers. "Huh?"

She shook her head. "You said the same thing earlier today."

Holden shrugged and sent her a lopsided smile. "Must have been the fever talking."

"What's your excuse now?"

"Temporary insanity."

Kayleigh whirled and headed toward the door. She stopped and spoke over her shoulder. "If I hear you fall in the shower, I'll call 9-1-1. So you better be super careful, or you'll be waiting a long time for help."

She heard Holden's chuckle as she pulled the door closed with a snap. If he knew what else he'd said while feverish, he'd be embarrassed.

form

Chapter 20

While Holden was in the bathroom, Kayleigh stripped the bed and quickly replaced the soiled sheets with clean ones. She tossed the wad of bedding into the hall. When did the housekeeper come? She thought it was on Friday, but it seemed rude to leave the bundle of laundry for Tara.

Holden opened the bathroom door holding a towel around his waist.

Kayleigh averted her eyes. "I'm going downstairs to get you some soup." She didn't wait for him to respond.

She warmed a bowl of chicken and dumplings for Holden and another for herself. Her stomach growled at the scent of the food. She put the rest of the pot in the refrigerator.

Balancing the two bowls, Kayleigh headed back up the stairs, noting again at the amount of exercise she'd been getting while taking care of Holden.

She found him sitting up in bed with two pillows behind his back. "Do you feel like you could eat something?"

Holden glanced up from his phone and nodded. "What is it?"

"It's my granny's famous chicken and dumplings."

"Famous where?"

Kayleigh shrugged. "Famous in our family circle, I guess."

Holden set his phone on the nightstand and reached for the bowl Kayleigh held. "It smells good."

"Wait until you taste it," Kayleigh said, perching on the edge of the wingback chair. She waited until Holden downed his first spoonful before she dug in. There was nothing in the world like Granny's chicken and dumplings.

"Tell me about your family," Holden said. His voice sounded rough, like sandpaper.

"Well, I'm an only child. My parents still live in Hornell, where I was born."

"I think I remember you telling me that. Friends?" Holden asked.

Kayleigh shrugged. "I've lost contact with a lot of friends from high school. Except for Samantha Jensen."

"The supermodel?"

Kayleigh sent him a questioning glance. "How do you know a supermodel?"

"I don't exactly know her. But I read about some stalker thing last year involving her and Logan Walters. Didn't they end up getting married?"

Kayleigh scooped the last dumpling piece from her bowl and spooned it into her mouth. "Yup. Sam is my best friend. As a matter of fact, she's staying at the Donaldson's and watching their dogs for me."

She watched Holden finish his soup and stood to take the empty bowl from him.

"How long have you been here?" Holden asked, his brow scrunched.

Kayleigh glanced at her phone for the time. It was

past three o'clock a.m. "About eighteen hours, give or take."

Holden's eyebrows rose. "I had no idea."

Kayleigh shrugged. "I guess it isn't in my job description, but I couldn't leave you alone to suffer."

Holden slid down under the covers, tossed one of the pillows aside and closed his eyes.

"My parents are coming tomorrow," he said. "They can relieve you of your duties."

Kayleigh regarded his still form. It hadn't been terrible, caring for this cranky pants. "How are you feeling?"

Holden coughed, gasping when the spasm stopped. "Awful. But at least the fever's gone."

"The doctor said to let him know if your breathing becomes labored."

Holden spoke with his eyes closed. "Go home. I'm fine."

"But—"

"No. Go home."

Kayleigh's face grew hot. How dare he dismiss her like a servant. After making him food, waiting for the doctor and the prescription, and he tells her to get lost?

The nerve.

If he wasn't still suffering, she'd tell him to take his attitude and his stupid admin job and shove it.

With one last glance back at Holden's still form, she strode from the room and out the back door to her waiting bed in the Donaldson's amazing guest room.

Luna and Rocky glanced up from their beds when she pushed open the back door. Samantha had left one light on over the stove to guide her way. She dragged herself up the stairs and into the bedroom. She shrugged out of her clothes and donned an oversized T-shirt and a pair of boxers.

The memory foam mattress embraced her, but sleep eluded her.

Darn Holden. Kayleigh felt like she'd gotten a glimpse into Holden's personality, but just like that, he'd reverted to his obnoxious ways.

While she tossed and turned, Kayleigh made the decision to stomp next door in the morning and tell Holden she quit.

Holden's phone dinged with a text the next morning, stirring him from an uneasy sleep. He'd been grateful Kayleigh had put clean sheets on the bed while he showered. But his conscience stabbed him all night with the way he'd dismissed her without saying even a tiny 'thank you.'

He was the worst person in the world.

His phone dinged again, seeming more insistent.

Mom: We're at your front door. Let us in.

Holden rubbed a hand over his face. His eyes felt gritty. Struggling to stand, Holden grabbed his cane and limped across the bedroom to the top of the stairs.

"You can do this," he said. His impulse was to turn around and fall back into bed. But his parents were waiting on his front porch.

He paused at the bottom of the stairs as a cough worked its way up from his belly. Still coughing, he opened the front door.

Mom was the first one in. She grabbed him in a hug, then grasped his upper arms and looked him up and down.

"You've lost weight."

"Let the boy go, Piper," Dad said.

Mom hugged him again and released him. Dad reached out a hand to grasp his, then pulled him into a hug.

Mom's brow creased with concern. "Dr. Sanders said you'd been ill."

Holden doubled over as coughing overtook him. His throat still felt raw, but not like it did yesterday.

"Let's go into the living room," Mom said. "You can lie down on the sofa and tell us all about it."

Holden let himself be pulled into the living room. Mom gently pushed him onto the sofa.

"Can I get you a throw?" she asked.

Holden nodded without speaking.

"I'll get you some water," Dad said, heading into the kitchen.

Mom laid a hand on his forehead and moved it to his cheek. "You don't feel hot. How are you?"

Holden adjusted a throw pillow under his head and laid an arm across his eyes. "Better."

"Oh, honey, I was so worried when Dr. Sanders called us. With your weakened immune system, he said you should never have gone to Thailand."

Holden groaned. He was an adult, for goodness' sake. Mom still treated him like he was ten.

"What if your cancer comes back?"

And there it was. The constant undertow of worry about his cancer, his general health, and his life expectancy. Things he dwelled on every single day. His parents shouldn't have to worry about him. Since Dad retired, they hadn't been able to enjoy their lives. And it was all his fault.

Maybe he'd die and put everyone out of their misery. Including him.

A knock on the back door broke the heavy silence. Mom stood and walked across the room to peer toward the screened-in porch.

"Holden, there's a pretty redhead at the door. How did she get into your backyard? And who is she?"

"Let her in," Holden said as Dad set a bottle of water in reach on the coffee table.

"But who is she?" Mom said.

"My temporary admin. She's staying next door."

"She's a looker," Dad said before sitting on the loveseat.

Holden had to agree. Even with his eyes closed, he knew when Kayleigh entered the room. She brought a sense of energy with her. And the fruity smell he recognized as Kayleigh's own signature scent.

Mom's voice was sharp when she addressed him. "Holden, at least say hello to Kayleigh."

Holden cracked one eye open and stifled a cough. "Kayleigh, these are my parents, Holden and Piper."

The leather creaked as Dad stood from the love seat. "Most people call me Mick. It's too confusing with two Holden Jeffries in the room."

"And when Granddad is with us, there's three."

"Nice to meet you," Kayleigh said. Holden heard hesitation in her voice.

"We flew up as soon as our doctor told us Holden was ill. I can't thank you enough for taking care of our boy."

Holden cringed. He was not a boy. But in Mom's mind, he was still a child who needed his parents.

"It was my pleasure," Kayleigh said.

Holden squeezed his eyes shut at the sight of Kayleigh wringing her hands. Why was she nervous? His parents were as down to earth as it gets, despite having built a real estate empire worth over a billion dollars.

"Well, since you're here," Kayleigh said. "I guess I'll go back to the Donaldson's"

"No, don't go," Mom said. "Sit and visit for a few minutes. It isn't often we get to meet one of Holden's friends."

Holden was too tired to argue with Mom, and to tell her he and Kayleigh weren't friends.

"I'll make coffee," Dad said.

"That would be great," Mom said. "Since you're the only one who knows how to use that fancy contraption disguised as a coffee maker."

Holden regarded Kayleigh through the slits of his barely opened eyes. Lying here on the sofa under a blanket, a cough tickling his throat, had him feeling vulnerable. And uncomfortable. And irritated. Why couldn't Mom just tell Kayleigh they had everything under control and send her home?

Instead, he was forced to listen to his mom charm his beautiful but untouchable temporary assistant.

JANE DALY

Chapter 21

Holden's parents were so sweet. Why hadn't their charming personalities rubbed off on their oldest child?

Kayleigh sipped the coffee Mick brought and answered Piper's questions about her life.

"I'm dog-sitting the Donaldsons' two pups."

"And after that? Where's home?" Piper asked.

Kayleigh hesitated. She had no firm plan for her life after this job.

"She's going back to Nashville," Holden said.

Kayleigh cut her gaze to Holden and back to his mom. "I haven't decided yet."

"Why Nashville?" Mick asked.

"She's a songwriter. And a singer," Holden said.

Kayleigh sent him a death glare, but his eyes were closed.

"Oh, how exciting," Piper said. "I'm the least musical person in the world." Her look turned wistful. "I tried piano lessons as a child, but I didn't have the discipline to pursue it." She shrugged. "I was more of a tomboy."

Kayleigh shifted her position, anxious to steer the conversation in a different direction. "So where do y'all live?"

Piper glanced at her husband and back at Kayleigh. "We have a place in the Thousand Islands."

Kayleigh tried to hide her expression of shock. Homes in the Thousand Islands of New York cost upwards of a million dollars.

"We live there in the summer and in Florida in the winter," Mick added. "We have a place in the City, but we rarely stay there."

"Too much noise and traffic," Piper said with a grimace.

Kayleigh shot a glance at Holden, who'd opened his eyes and looked amused.

"Are you from New York?" Piper asked.

"I was born and raised in Hornell."

"Oh, that's a darling little town," Piper said, not in the least condescending. "We used to have an Air B&B there, until someone made us an offer we couldn't refuse, and we sold it."

Kayleigh fought the urge to jump to her feet and make a mad dash toward the door. She was way out of her element. One glance at Piper's soft linen slacks and designer top were enough to make her want to hide her Walmart shorts and T-shirt.

"Holden's sister, Jenna, said she met you last week."

"Uh-huh. And Andrew too."

Piper glanced at Mick. "We'd hoped Andrew would also want to be a part of the family business, but he had his own ideas."

Kayleigh could relate. Her parents often reminded her that trying to make a go in the music industry was like trying to get into the NBA. They were disappointed she didn't want to become an accountant like her dad and become part of his firm.

Mick set his coffee cup down. "Now, Piper, honey, you know we've always encouraged the kids to forge their own paths."

Piper exhaled a wistful sigh. "I know. I just wish one of the three would settle down and give me some grandkids."

Kayleigh saw Holden wince. Didn't his parents know about his little problem? She set her empty cup next to Mick's. "I better get back to the Donaldson's. I think my friend is tired of doing my job as dog-sitter."

Kayleigh rose from her set. Piper stood and pulled her into a warm hug. "Thank you so much for taking care of Holden. I'd like to do something nice to pay you back."

"That's not necessary. But thank you." Kayleigh pulled back and stared into Piper's blue eyes. The same color of Holden's gaze. But hers was kind whereas his was not.

Piper smiled. "I'll think of something."

"Again, not necessary."

Kayleigh looked down at Holden. His eyes were open and clear, unlike when he'd bared his fever-wracked soul with glazed eyes.

"Let me know if you have any work for me." As soon as the words came out of her mouth, she wanted to snatch them back. She'd come over this morning to quit, and instead was pulled into his parents' warmth.

Kayleigh loved her parents, but they didn't have the same acceptance of her life choices as the Jeffries seemed to have. Andrew, who spent his days chartering fishing expeditions, and Jenna who was building an event planning business.

Still, her parents loved her unconditionally. Maybe it was time to explore some career options other than music.

Holden's deep voice interrupted her train of thought. "I'll make a list for you for tomorrow." He coughed and looked drained when the fit was over. "I'm behind on emails and such."

Piper's face creased with worry. She followed Kayleigh out the door and into the humid morning.

She grasped Kayleigh's arm and pulled her to a stop outside the door. "I'm worried about Holden. Dr. Sanford said he needs to take it easy for at least a week, maybe longer." She hesitated. "Would it be too much for you to keep an eye on him?"

Kayleigh wanted to say yes, it would be too much. But the concern in Piper's voice and the stiffness of her posture had Kayleigh saying, "No, I'm happy to help."

Piper's shoulders dropped. "Thank you. It's obvious Holden cares for you. Do you feel the same way?"

How to respond to that? Sure, Holden was handsome. And charming when he wanted to be. Kayleigh remembered when he'd laughed when she thought Jenna was his girlfriend. She did care for him in a biblical 'love your neighbor' kind of way.

She was kidding herself. Her feelings for Holden were more complicated. He ticked all the boxes. Family focused, handsome, single. But emotionally unavailable. Any attraction on her part was sure to end in a broken heart.

When Kayleigh didn't immediately answer, Piper continued. "I know he can be a bit prickly. Before his cancer, Holden was a lot, how should I say this? Um, relaxed."

"Hm."

"He's convinced himself no woman could possibly be interested in him. Partly because of the diagnosis. I mean, no one knows how long they'll live, right?"

Kayleigh suppressed a shudder. Why was Holden's mom sharing intimate details of her son's life to a virtual stranger?

"And also because the doctors told him he might not be able to have children due to the radiation he received in his hip." Piper leaned closer. "Because of the proximity of his, you know." Piper's face suffused with color.

Kayleigh wanted to press her for more information. But how awkward to be talking about Holden's reproductive capabilities with his mom.

Kayleigh swallowed. "So he *could* have kids?"

Piper nodded. 'It's possible. But he's convinced himself otherwise." She sighed. "Men are so annoying." She smiled and Kayleigh smiled back.

What would a couple of little Holdens look like? Ice-blue eyes for sure. Dark hair or red like hers? So many possible combinations.

"I just want my kids to be happy, you know?" Piper said. "To settle down and give me some grandchildren."

Why did it seem like every parent wants grandkids? Even her own folks brought up the subject from time to time.

When Holden heard his mom follow Kayleigh out the back door, he wished he was strong enough to follow them and pull Kayleigh away from his mom. No telling what nonsense she was telling the beautiful redhead.

"I'm sorry, Son. I didn't ask if you wanted some coffee?" Dad stood and retrieved the empty cups from the coffee table.

"I'm fine, Dad. Maybe some more 7-Up if there's any left."

"Holden, you'd tell me if there was anything going on between you and your assistant, wouldn't you?"

Holden answered through gritted teeth. "Sure, Dad. You'll be the first to know."

"I don't appreciate your sarcasm." Dad looked down at him. "I saw the way you looked at her. Like you wanted to sweep her away from us. I can't help but wonder why."

Holden was saved from answering by his mom returning to the house.

"What a lovely young lady," she said.

"Come into the kitchen with me, honey, and I'll show you how to use Holden's fancy espresso machine."

Holden had no doubt his parents would whisper about Kayleigh out of earshot. They'd been trying to get him to date since he and his last girlfriend broke up. Friends of friends. Daughters of friends of friends. Someone's cousin. He'd had so many women thrown at him he'd lost count.

His parents would have a better chance of grandchildren by focusing on Jenna and Andrew. Why bring a child into the world whose father might die in five years? That wasn't something he wanted to wish on any woman.

Mom returned to the living room carrying a fresh

cup of coffee. "I had a little chat with Kayleigh."

Holden groaned.

"Don't be like that, Holden. Kayleigh has agreed to make sure you're taking it easy."

Holden struggled to a sitting position. His head swum for a moment before settling. "Mom, in case you haven't noticed, I'm twenty-nine years old. Which means I'm an adult. Have you not kept track of my birthdays?"

"Pfft. Of course I have. But I also know what a workaholic you are. Dad and I have discussed it. He is going to take care of the upcoming board meeting. You and he will go through the elder care home proposal and take the decision to the board."

Holden groaned. He loved his parents, but since his cancer, they'd hovered like an aggressive bumble bee.

Holden's dad set a frosty glass of bubbly liquid on the coffee table. "Here's your 7-Up."

"Thanks, Dad." If he thought he'd get his dad on his side, he was dead wrong.

"Your mom and I have it all worked out. You and I will get some work done today as long as you feel up to it, and your mom will make sure you have food to eat."

Holden held his head with both hands. He might as well quit trying to argue. On his own, his dad was a force to be reckoned with. Along with Mom, they formed a ten-foot-high brick wall. One which he was too weak to breach.

"Fine."

Now to find out what his mom had said to Kayleigh.

JANE DALY

Chapter 22

While his dad went upstairs to retrieve Holden's laptop, and his mom went to the kitchen, Holden sent a text to Kayleigh.

Holden: I apologize for my parents.

He waited for the dots to appear showing Kayleigh was tapping out a response.

Kayleigh: They're sweet
Holden: Nosy
Kayleigh: Aren't all parents? I think it's in the parental contract.

This was followed by a laughing emoji.

Holden tapped the phone against his chin, thinking about his response.

Holden: Are your parents the same?
Kayleigh: Are you kidding me? Mine want me to become a CPA

She added the 'smack my forehead' emoji

Holden laughed.

Holden: Somehow I can't picture you crunching numbers in some soulless office
Kayleigh: I know, right? I don't have any pockets to put a pocket protector in
Holden: Such a shame

There was a thirty second pause before she responded.
Kayleigh: Why are you being so nice?
Holden: It must be the fever
Kayleigh: Liar. Your fever broke last night, remember?
Holden: Don't worry, I'll revert to my snarky self next time I see you
Kayleigh: IF I return that is
Holden sent the praying hands emoji. Please don't quit.
Kayleigh's response was the shrugging emoji.
His stomach sank. As soon as he was well, Kayleigh would probably tell him to go somewhere the sun didn't shine. And he'd never see her again.
Why did the thought depress him so much?

Kayleigh hugged Samantha goodbye on the front porch.
"I'm going to miss you, Sam. I feel like I hardly got to see you."
Sam smirked. "You were too busy taking care of Mr. Cranky Pants." She waggled her eyebrows. "Nothing like seeing someone sick to learn more about them."
Kayleigh rolled her eyes. "If I hadn't promised his mom, I'd tell him I quit."
"Oh, honey, don't do that."
"We'll see."
"I'll come back before you finish your doggie job here, okay?"
"That would be awesome. I promise to spend more

time with you than with," Kayleigh flipped a hand in the direction of Holden's house.

"Don't make promises you can't keep." Sam pulled her into another hug as the Town Car pulled into the driveway. "There's my ride. Love you."

"I love you too. Bye."

The house felt cavernous and too quiet after Sam's departure. "C'mon, guys, let's go for a walk."

At the word 'walk,' Luna and Rocky jumped to their feet, tongues hanging out. Kayleigh clipped on their leashes, grabbed the mailbox key, and headed out the front door.

She inhaled the humid air smelling of the pine and spruce trees lining the long driveway. Birds sang as they flitted from branch to branch. Kayleigh envied them. Their music flowed instinctively from inside them. Unlike her. She struggled to get every word right, every note perfect.

Was she too hard on herself? Should she lighten up and go back to when she was a child and wrote silly songs to entertain and delight her folks? After Gary Golden, she'd never trust anyone in the music business again.

Kayleigh's thoughts turned to the text exchange with Holden. He'd been funny. So not in his character. Maybe he was still under the influence of a fever. Added to what his mom had revealed, it would be too easy to fall for texting Holden. But not real-life Holden.

She retrieved the mail and returned to the house.

Granny's letter sat on top of the Donaldson's mail. What had Granny sent?

She released the dogs, and they loped to their water dishes and slurped noisily. Kayleigh plopped the mail on top of the stack she'd set on the kitchen island. Running her finger under the envelope flap, she tore open the letter from Granny.

A couple of lottery tickets fluttered to the floor. Granny's letter was short.

My dear Kayleigh,

I haven't told your parents yet, but my health is getting worse. Please don't worry about me. I know where I'm going after I leave this world. I hope you have the same confidence.

Anyway, I bought these lottery tickets on a whim when I was with your Mama at your aunt's birthday party scavenger hunt. I think it's all nonsense, but who knows? You might win a couple of dollars.

I hope when you finish your dog-sitting job, you'll come home for a spell. I'd love to have some sweet tea and sugar cookies with you. You can give me an update on your music.

Love,

Granny

Kayleigh swallowed a sob. What did Granny mean, her health was getting worse? She hadn't known Granny was sick. A stab of guilt pierced her chest. She should have made more of an effort to visit home.

Was this a sign from God that she should stop pursuing a career in music? If she moved back home, she could attend a local community college. She could visit Granny more often. And maybe relieve Mom and Dad of some of their caregiving duties.

If only she had a sibling or two to carry part of the burden. Which turned her thoughts to Holden and his brother and sister. How odd to be a set of triplets. They seemed very close. Did they know Holden had been

sick? Probably. Piper would have informed them. Holden's folks were sweet. Kayleigh was especially taken with Holden's mom. It was still a little cringy that Piper had shared about Holden's ability to have children.
And what did she mean, 'no one knows how long they'll live.' Was Holden dying?
It was all too much. Granny, Holden, Gary Golden ...
Time for a nap.
Kayleigh woke from her nap with a new song rumbling around in her head. She grabbed her notebook and guitar and headed to the back porch.
The patio overhang shielded her from the afternoon sun. She set the notebook and pencil on the table and strummed her guitar.
It was a breakup song. She wrote 'Wrong Kind of Pretty On A Saturday Night' on a new sheet.
Dressing up going out on a Saturday night
Gonna make a little trouble, maybe start a little fight
Gonna flirt with the boys and maybe kiss one or two
Oh yeah, baby, that's what I'm gonna do
Cuz I'm the wrong kind of pretty on a Saturday night

Don't need no Carrie Underwood
No one's gonna tell me to be good
Got better plans than a bat or a key
I'll make you wish you were still with me
Red lips, High heels, and a skirt so tight
I'll be the wrong kind of pretty on a Saturday night

She chewed on the end of the pencil, then wrote some notes down over the words. Repeating the process, Kayleigh lost track of time as she created a new song.

Sometime later, the sun had sunk close to the horizon. Kayleigh raised her arms over her head and stretched. Rocky and Luna had found a place to snooze in the shade on one side of the lawn.

Kayleigh stood and bent over to stretch the kinks from her back. The dogs raised their heads and looked expectantly at her.

"What do you want?" Kayleigh asked. She picked up a tennis ball from the deck and waved it in their direction. "Is this what you want?"

The dogs raced toward her and stood with their tails wagging. Kayleigh hurled the ball and laughed when Rocky and Luna raced each other to retrieve it.

When her arm grew tired, Kayleigh called the dogs into the house and prepared their supper. She took her own meal outside to enjoy the evening breeze cooling the day. From her vantage point, she caught a glimpse of Seneca Lake. The sliver of water glimmered like a black opal.

With a glance back to see the dogs lounging on their beds after scarfing their meal, Kayleigh strode down the sloping yard, through the fence, and to the lake's edge.

She meandered along the shore until she reached a dock. Glancing away from the water, she realized she'd walked to the edge of Holden's property.

The low hum of a boat motor caught her attention. A fishing boat slowed as it reached the deck.

"Hey!" a man called. "Grab this rope." He tossed a rope from the bow.

Kayleigh caught it. "What do you want me to do with it?"

"Hold it for a minute."

The voice was familiar. Like Holden's, but slightly different.

Andrew.

He jumped from the boat and took the rope from her hand. "Thanks."

After he secured the bow and the stern by lashing the rope to the cleats mounted on the deck, he turned to face her.

"What a nice surprise to find you waiting for me."

JANE DALY

Chapter 23

Not long after Mom and Dad left, Andrew showed up at the back door.

"Hey, Bro, heard you were on your deathbed."

Holden addressed his brother from his spot on the sofa. "Hardly."

"To hear Mom tell it, you require 24/7 nursing." Andrew spread his arms. "That's why I'm here."

Holden sent him a sardonic smile. "You're the worst nurse in the universe."

Andrew shoved Holden's feet off the sofa and plopped down. "I ran into your admin down at the dock. Perhaps she would be willing to nurse you back to health."

Holden's pulse spiked. What was Kayleigh doing at his dock? Did she and Andrew plan to meet? Andrew was a chick-magnet. His charm reeled in more than the fish people paid him to find. Married, single, old, young—it didn't matter. Every female longed to be pulled into Andrew's orbit.

Holden coughed, the spasm doubling him over. When the spasm passed, his voice was raspy. "What was she doing at my dock?"

Andrew raised his eyebrows. "Why? Are you

jealous?"

"No." *Yes*. The last thing he wanted was to see his brother make a move on Kayleigh. Holden was like a toddler with a toy. He didn't want the toy, but he didn't want anyone else to have it.

Andrew stretched his arms above his head. "Good. Because she is smokin' hot. I'm gonna ask her out."

Holden's jaw tightened. He'd have to come up with a plan to keep Kayleigh away from his brother.

Weariness overtook him after the day of working with his dad. "I'm going up to bed," he said, struggling to his feet. "Make yourself at home."

Andrew grinned. "I always do."

Holden swallowed the antibiotic and downed some cough suppressant, then fell into bed. This time, no dreams of Kayleigh or anything else kept him from a deep sleep.

Around three o'clock, Holden woke to a coughing fit. He padded into the bathroom and downed a tepid glass of water. Was it only last night Kayleigh had brought him ice cold 7-Up? He vaguely remembered mumbling some nonsense while his fever raged. Had he embarrassed himself?

Ugh.

He fell back into bed and slept until the sunlight peeked through the edges of the plantation shutters. He needed coffee. The smell of the delicious brew wafted up the stairs. Using his cane for support, Holden descended the stairs and entered the kitchen. Andrew had brewed a traditional pot of coffee using the Cuisinart Grind and Brew.

Holden sniffed appreciatively and poured himself a cup. He carried it into the living room. Voice drew him to the back porch. His temper flared when he spied Andrew and Kayleigh sitting across from each other at one of the patio tables. Andrew leaned forward and said something to Kayleigh that made her laugh.

"I'm going to put my number in your phone. You know, in case you have a sudden urge to join me on my boat."

Holden stepped through the door. "What's going on out here?"

Kayleigh's face flushed deep red.

Andrew sat back in his chair. "Good morning, H. How are you feeling today?"

Holden's grip tightened on his cane. He resisted the urge to swing it at his brother's head.

Kayleigh pushed her chair back. "Do you have some work for me today?"

Holden scowled. "Looks like my brother has kept you occupied."

Andrew laughed. "Drink your coffee, H. You need some caffeine to turn you into a human."

Kayleigh snickered, covering her mouth.

"I'm gonna go get a refill," Andrew said, pushing himself to his feet. "Sure I can't get you something?" He directed this remark to Kayleigh, who shook her head.

Holden sat on the chair Andrew vacated. He was uncomfortably aware he wore only a T-shirt and a pair of boxers. He took a sip of coffee and regarded Kayleigh over the rim.

"Be careful of getting involved with my brother."

Kayleigh sent him a death glare. "What business is it of yours?"

A tickle worked its way up from Holden's chest and

ended in a coughing spasm.

Kayleigh reached out an arm. "Can I get you some water or something?"

Holden shook his head. When the coughing spell subsided, he took a long drink of lukewarm coffee. His voice was raspy when he spoke.

"All I'm saying is that Andrew is a player." He swallowed the rest of the words he wanted to say. Andrew was his twin, after all.

"Thanks for the warning. But I'll take my chances."

Holden's jaw tightened. It would kill him to see his brother hook up with Kayleigh. On one hand, he wanted to grab her and whisk her away from Andrew's influence. On the other hand, what could he possibly offer her?

It was time for some serious self-reflection.

Kayleigh regarded Holden through lowered eyelids. Why was he so ornery? Andrew was only being nice, offering her a ride on his boat.

She nudged Rocky, who reclined under the glass-topped patio table. Her gaze was caught by Holden's bare legs and feet. He and Andrew might be twins, but Holden was much thinner. She guessed it was from his cancer treatment.

Instead of being annoyed with him, she decided to show Holden some grace. Having to deal with cancer must be horrible at such a young age. According to his Wikipedia page, Holden was twenty-nine years old. Too young to think about dying.

Her voice softened. "Are you feeling any better today?"

"Not really."

"I'm sorry. Is there anything I can do?" Kayleigh noted Holden's pale face and dark circles under his eyes.

"My dad I and did some work yesterday. I left a list on my desk of a few things I need you to do."

Kayleigh nodded. Good, Holden seemed to have lost his adversarial attitude.

Until he spoke again. "If you can pull away from my brother, that is."

And there it was. Back to Mr. Cranky Pants.

Kayleigh got to her feet and rested her hands on the table. She leaned forward. "Look, I am done with you being cranky to me. You act like I'm your worst enemy. Did you forget I stayed with you all night when you were feverish? Did you forget I changed your sweat-soaked sheets while you took a shower? And that I made you chicken and dumplings?"

She straightened. "Until you can treat me with respect and kindness, I'm going home. Well, back to the Donaldson's."

She whistled for the dogs and strode across the patio to the gate. Her hand shook as she latched the gate behind her.

The nerve of him. Kayleigh reached the Donaldson's back door. The spike of adrenaline seeped out, leaving her weak.

What had she done? She'd thrown away the opportunity to make a pile of money before her gig here ended. Why did her temper seem to get the better of her? Especially where Holden was concerned. Before she could talk herself out of it, she sent a text to Andrew.

Kayleigh: I'd love to take you up on your offer for a boat ride.

Take that, Mr. Cranky Pants.

She plopped onto the sofa and pulled her computer onto her lap. A new email hit her inbox.

Ms. McGuire,

My name is Oliver Young, and I represent Young Music. I heard you perform at Sidekick Bar and Restaurant several weeks ago in Nashville. I'd like to schedule an appointment with you to discuss your potential future in the music industry.

Please respond to this email with some times you are available for a Zoom call.

Sincerely, Oliver Young, Executive Producer and Agent, Young Music

Kayleigh read and reread the email. Another scam like Gary Golden? Her finger hovered over the delete key. Word must have gotten around Nashville that she was an easy mark. Her stomach did a curlicue. What if this was legit?

She shook her head. Nope. Not gonna fall for it a second time. She hit delete.

Her phone dinged with an incoming text.

Andrew: Meet me at the dock in an hour. I'll take you for a ride.

Kayleigh's nerves tingled in anticipation of spending time with a handsome—and nice—man. He and Holden might be identical in looks, but their personalities were eons apart. So why did she wish it was Holden who was taking her out on his boat?

Chapter 24

Holden stood in his bedroom window and watched Andrew prepare his boat. Was his brother leaving already? They hadn't spoken since Kayleigh had flounced off in a huff. Holden had returned upstairs, exhaustion pulling at him.

A few minutes later, Kayleigh appeared into view. Andrew pulled her into a hug. He released her, and they climbed into Andrew's boat and backed away from the deck.

Holden ground his teeth in frustration. Andrew's MO was to date a woman two times—no more—and ghost them. He was a serial dater with a slew of broken hearts left in the wake of his sleek fishing boat.

Holden couldn't let that happen to Kayleigh.

"I shouldn't care. It's obvious she hates me." His voice echoed in the empty bedroom.

Holden crashed onto the bed. His head ached and his throat was on fire. He'd take a nap and call Dr. Sanford.

He glanced over at the wing chair where Kayleigh had spent the night keeping an eye on him. He should be grateful for her care. He was grateful.

You have a crappy way of showing it.

His conscience pricked whenever he remembered his harsh words. Was it too late to make amends with her? It was easier to keep others, especially women, Kayleigh in particular, at arms' length. Letting others close only meant more heartache when he died.

Sure, Dr. Sanford and the oncology team promised him a long life. If—and it was a big if—his scans stayed clear of cancer for the next five years.

His body was a ticking time bomb. He could die before he turned thirty-five. What kind of life was that to offer Kayleigh. Or any woman.

A tiny voice whispered in his brain. *What if she wants to take a chance on you?*

Holden fell asleep with that thought echoing in his conscience.

When he woke, his chest felt like he'd been hit with a baseball bat. He reached for his phone and sent a text to Dr. Sanford asking for a phone call.

Holden splashed water on his face and decided he was too tired to take a shower. Instead, he pulled on a pair of athletic shorts, noticing how they slid down his hips.

Food. That might take the boulder off his chest. He remembered Kayleigh had made some chicken soup with some homemade noodles or something. He hoped she'd left them in his fridge.

She had, and Holden warmed a bowl in the microwave. He carried it out to the back deck, noticing the absence of Andrew's boat. Sibling rivalry raised its head as Holden remembered how Andrew had hugged Kayleigh when she'd stepped onto the dock.

Don't kid yourself. It was not sibling rivalry. It was jealousy plain and simple.

The sound of a boat motor wafted toward him. Holden watched as Andrew trolled into the small cove at the end of his property. Kayleigh wore a baseball cap with a cascade of hair spilling through the hole in the back of the cap. What would that silky hair feel like spilling over his hands?

Andrew secured his boat to the dock and reached out to help Kayleigh clamber out of the boat. Holden's lips tightened when Andrew didn't release Kayleigh's hand once she was safely on the dock.

Be nice, he told himself.

Holden forced his expression into neutral as the pair walked up the hill from the water's edge to where Holden sat. Kayleigh frowned when she caught sight of him.

"Hey, Bro, did you have a nice nap?" Andrew asked.

"Yes, thank you for asking," Holden replied.

Kayleigh's face showed surprise at his response. "I see you're eating some of my Granny's chicken and dumplings."

"Yes, they taste great."

"Granny always said they're better the second day."

Holden raised his spoon. "Your granny is correct."

Andrew sniffed the air, inhaling the scent of the chicken soup. "I'm gonna go get me some of that. Want any?" he asked Kayleigh.

"No, thank you, I should get back and check on Luna and Rocky."

Holden wanted to keep her there longer, but he understood her need to check on the dogs. "Thank you for making this," he said, pointing to the bowl.

She sent him a questioning look. "You're

welcome."

Holden sucked in a breath, struggling with the pressure in his chest. His tongue felt thick as he tried to form words. Not since he was in third grade had a girl caused him to be so tongue-tied.

"Um, if you want to use the pool, to swim, you can bring the dogs with you."

Kayleigh's gaze narrowed with suspicion. "Okay. Thanks."

"I'll probably be upstairs working, or something ..." his voice trailed off. He didn't want her to think he'd be watching her swim. Although the thought of seeing her again in a swimsuit spiked his pulse. He was like a lovesick teenager.

"I'll think about it," Kayleigh said. "Please tell Andrew I said thanks."

Andrew appeared at the back door. "Thanks for what?"

"For the boat ride. That was fun."

"We can go again tomorrow," Andrew said.

Holden pushed his spoon into the nearly empty bowl. "I thought you came to nurse me back to health."

Andrew laughed. "I can do both. Anyway, I'll probably head out tomorrow afternoon. I have clients stacked up wanting me to take them fishing."

Holden felt guilty and relieved at the same time. He and Andrew were close as could be, but he was glad his brother would be out of the way. He had some serious making up to do to keep Kayleigh coming to work, and Andrew would only be in the way.

"Well, thanks again. I better get going."

Both men watched as Kayleigh disappeared into the hedge.

Andrew gave a low whistle. "Whoa. What a babe. Too bad I can't stick around." He set his bowl of soup on the table and plopped into a chair.

"Yeah, too bad." Holden couldn't help the sarcasm dripping off his words.

"You like her," Andrew said. "Are you crushing on your temporary assistant?"

Holden wanted to smack the grin off his brother's face. He opened his mouth to respond, then snapped it closed. Of course, Andrew knew what he was thinking. He always did.

"So what if I am?"

Andrew didn't respond. He just grinned.

Kayleigh felt unsettled and restless when she returned from the boat ride with Andrew. He'd been all charm and friendliness, putting an arm around her shoulders while he pointed out the homes of famous people who lived on Seneca Lake.

Returning to the house, Holden was actually nice. *Nice.* Had he had a personality transplant while she was with Andrew?

Then, there was the letter from Granny and the email from some random 'music producer.' Sheesh. Too much drama.

Kayleigh pushed the speed dial on her phone to call her mother.

"What a nice surprise, Kayleigh," said Mom, answering on the first ring.

"Hi, Mom. How are you and Dad?"

"We're fine, honey. What's new with you?"

Kayleigh chewed on a fingernail. "How's Granny?"

"She's fine. Why do you ask?"

"I got her letter, and she said something about not having long to live."

Surprisingly, Mom laughed. "Oh, Kayleigh, your grandmother been saying that for years."

"So she's not dying?"

"Heavens no. Her heart may be a little weak, and she has issues with her balance, but she'll probably outlive us all."

Kayleigh exhaled. "Okay. Well, that's a relief. She sent me a couple of lottery tickets. What was that all about?"

"I have no idea. Your grandmother sometimes does some odd things. Who knows, maybe you'll be a winner."

"Doubtful. Anyway, I wanted to talk to you about something." She sucked in a breath through her nose and blew it out. "When I'm done dog-sitting, I thought I might come home. If that's all right with you."

"Of course." Mom's voice was enthusiastic. "You don't have to ask."

"Great. Thanks. I'm not sure how long, though. I'm thinking about maybe going back to college."

It was time to let her dream die. A spark of a song had her grabbing a pencil and turning to a fresh page in her notebook. She wrote, 'Letting My Dream Die.'

Mom's voice cut in. "Kay? Where'd you go?"

"Sorry, Mom. I got distracted for a moment." Suddenly, she wanted to end the call with Mom and jot down some lyrics. "Mom, I have to go. I'll call you in a couple of days."

Tucking her legs under her, Kayleigh began to write.

I thought we'd last forever
I thought we'd find a way
I thought I'd found the one
But then I knew
that I had to go.

That lipstick on your shoulder
That perfume on your skin
That secret smile when you thought I didn't see
Made me know
That it was time to leave
Time to let the dream of us die

It was rough, but a start. She tapped the pencil against her teeth, wondering again if she'd been premature in deleting the email from that guy, Oliver Young.

A search of the internet showed a professional-looking website, along with several testimonials from some well-known artists.

The doorbell rang. Kayleigh tossed her pencil and notebook on the sofa and rose to answer it.

An older man stood on the porch holding a box.

"Food delivery for Sandra Donaldson," he said.

"Awesome. Let me take that." Kayleigh reached for the box. "Thank you."

The man took a clipboard from under his arm and handed it to her. "Sign here, please."

Kayleigh rested the clipboard on the box and realized she wouldn't be able to hold the box with one arm.

"Let me grab that," the man said. They wrestled

with the shipment and the clipboard until Kayleigh was able to sign the form.

"Thanks again," she said.

The man tipped an imaginary hat and returned to the white panel van idling in the driveway. Kayleigh carried the box to the kitchen and slit it open. Sandra had ordered enough meals to last for a week. If she was a family of seven. That was a lot of food.

Her thoughts turned to Holden, living alone next door. She pulled the flap back and peered into the box. Plenty to share.

But did she dare enter the lion's den again? Which Holden would greet her? Friendly Holden? Or beastly Holden?

Time to find out.

Chapter 25

Holden didn't expect to see Kayleigh again when she knocked on the back door. He'd been resting on the sofa. Andrew had disappeared into the basement, no doubt watching a movie in the media center.

He clambered to his feet and waved her in. She carried a reusable grocery bag.

Holding the bag aloft, she said, "I brought some food to share. Sandra ordered enough for a party of fifty."

Holden took a moment to admire her legs. From her red hair cascading over her shoulders, to her flip-flop clad feet, Kayleigh was the whole package. Feisty, pretty, and artistic. His breath caught.

"Well?" Kayleigh asked. "Do you want food or not?"

"Yes, please." Holden pointed to the kitchen and followed her. "How much preparation do you have to do?"

He leaned against the counter and watched her unpack the bag.

"Not much. How do you turn on your oven?"

Holden shrugged. "I have no idea. You're looking at someone who's helpless in the kitchen."

Kayleigh sent him a sardonic grin. "Why does that not surprise me."

Holden felt the edges of his mouth turn up into a grin. "Let's see if we can figure it out." He stood shoulder to shoulder with Kayleigh in front of the double oven. She fiddled with the knobs and buttons, poking them with calloused fingers. Holden had a brief memory of those fingers on his forehead and cheek.

He took a step back and swallowed. "I think you're cracked the code."

"Yay. I'll preheat the oven and put these containers in to bake. The instructions said it will take twenty minutes."

Holden nodded.

Kayleigh turned from the oven and said, "What do you want to do while the oven preheats?"

Holden could think of a lot of things he'd like to do in the next twenty minutes. The main thing would be to pull Kayleigh close and kiss those full, red lips.

Reality smacked him in the face. He looked like something one of her dogs had dragged in from the lake. He hadn't showered and his breath probably smelled like he'd swallowed a dragon.

"I'll go sit in the living room." Holden's throat tightened.

He heard the clatter of silverware and dishes and assumed Kayleigh was setting the table. Holden hoped Andrew would stay downstairs so he could eat with Kayleigh alone.

His hopes were dashed when Andrew climbed up the stairs from the basement. "Great movie, H. You would have liked it."

Holden doubted it. As much as his brother and he

were carbon copies of each other, their tastes in music, books, and movies were polar opposite.

"Who's here?" Andrew asked.

"Kayleigh brought dinner." Holden waited for Andrew's snarky response. He didn't have to wait long.

"Nice move, Bro. How'd you manage to lure her back?"

"There was no luring involved. She came of her own free will."

Kayleigh's voice rang out from the kitchen. "I can hear you, you know."

Holden and Andrew exchanged a grin.

"Oops," Andrew whispered.

Kayleigh stuck her head out of the kitchen. "Hi, Andrew. I didn't know you were still here."

"I'm leaving tomorrow," Andrew said. He cut a glance toward Holden. "I can take you out for a ride again tomorrow before I leave."

Holden sent Andrew a look that he hoped would shut him up. His stomach did a barrel roll when Kayleigh said, "No, thank you. I'm pretty sure Holden has work for me to do."

Holden couldn't read her expression, but hope bloomed in his chest. Maybe Kayleigh didn't hate him after all. And Andrew couldn't pull her into his orbit.

Kayleigh stood and watched the two brothers for a moment. So alike and yet so different. Andrew exuded a laid-back charm, while Holden was Type A all the way. She had to ask herself why she kept coming back here when Holden had been rude and demanding.

Because her heart had softened toward him. Not

with pity, although pity lurked in the shadows. How terrible to face a crippling diagnosis like cancer at such a young age.

Sadness pushed against her chest as she considered what Piper had told her. 'None of us knows how long we have to live.'

With a shake of her head, Kayleigh returned to the kitchen to retrieve another place setting for Andrew.

The oven dinged its announcement that the oven had preheated. She shoved the containers of meat loaf and mashed potatoes into the oven and set the timer on her phone. One of the cupboards yielded a bowl large enough to throw together a salad.

She paused inside the doorway from the kitchen to the dining room, hoping to eavesdrop on the guys. Their voices were low, but she caught pieces of their conversation.

"Remember when we were little and we had our own language?" Andrew asked.

Holden laughed. "It drove Jenna crazy."

"And Mom too. Dad said we'd grow out of it. I guess we did."

Kayleigh's heart warmed. How sweet the two were still close. How many times had she wished for a brother or sister? What would she be like if she'd grown up with siblings?

Ah, well. That ship sailed a long time ago. When she got married, Kayleigh wanted a big family. Three or four kids, all two years apart. She imagined little Holden clones, with dark hair and blue eyes. Or girls with her red hair and pale skin. Shaking herself from a stupid daydream, she returning to the kitchen to check on dinner.

"A few more minutes," Kayleigh called from the kitchen.

Get hold of yourself, girlfriend. Holden is emotionally unavailable.

So why was she falling for him?

The guys kept Kayleigh entertained during dinner with stories of their childhood shenanigans. Kayleigh laughed until tears sprouted from the corners of her eyes.

She wiped her eyes with a napkin "Your parents must have been at their wit's end."

Andrew threw a sideways glance at Holden. "You don't know the half of it."

Kayleigh's heart caught in her throat when Holden grinned at her. His smile deepened the dimple in his chin. Another dimple made its appearance in the stubble on his cheeks.

"We've given you the sanitized version of our misbehaving. We did some stuff in middle school that I'm still ashamed of."

"That piques my interest," Kayleigh said.

"What about you," Andrew asked. "What kind of misdeeds did you participate in?"

Kayleigh shook her head. "I have nothing to confess. I was the proverbial 'good girl.' The worst thing I ever did was write a song about one of our least favorite teachers and publish it in the school newspaper." Her face warmed as she remembered being called to the principal's office and being forced to publicly apologize to that teacher.

"Oh, so our good girl has a wild side," Holden teased. "Good to know."

Andrew leaned toward Holden and said in a mock

whisper, "Watch your back, Bro."

Kayleigh pressed her lips together to keep from smiling. Tonight's dinner was the most fun she'd had in a long time. This must be what it was like having brothers. Bantering around the dinner table, reminiscing about childhood drama, is what she'd missed growing up as an only child.

Dinner talk in her home had been about politics, current events, and finances. As a CPA, Dad constantly hammered the importance of fiscal responsibility. She dreaded telling her parents that Gary Golden had robbed her.

Kayleigh pushed back her chair and gathered their empty plates. "I'll take these to the kitchen."

Andrew stood. "Let me help you."

Kayleigh felt a stab of disappointment that Holden didn't offer. But of course, he'd have a difficult time trying to carry dishes in one hand and his cane in the other. Plus, he still looked pale and shaky.

"I'll be on the back patio, enjoying the evening breeze while you two slave over the dishes." Holden stood and made his way out the back door.

Andrew took the dinner plates from Kayleigh's hands. "Go outside. I've got this." He sent her a knowing wink.

Kayleigh's face grew hot. Was it that obvious that she was starting to like Holden?

Chapter 26

Holden stretched out on one of the padded loungers and pulled in a lungful of humid summer air. In less than an hour, the breeze would turn cool, and the air would be fresh.

Kayleigh's steps approached where he lay with his eyes closed.

"Do you mind if I let the dogs come over?"

"Sure." Holden enjoyed the feel of Luna and Rocky resting on his feet when they'd sat at the table yesterday. They'd never grown up with pets. Although he had a distant memory of Jenna begging for a gerbil.

Weariness pressed Holden back against the lounger. Maybe tomorrow he'd have a tiny bit of energy after Dr. Sanford paid a visit.

The Donaldson's dogs burst through the hedge and dashed toward him. He pushed open his eyes and patted them on the head. "Hey, fur balls."

Once they'd received their dose of attention, they headed toward the far end of the property to sniff the bushes.

Kayleigh sat on a lounger next to him. "Your view of the lake is better than mine."

Holden's gaze focused on Kayleigh rather than the

glimmering water in the distance. "My view is pretty fantastic."

She turned to face him. Holden smothered a grin when two rosy spots appeared on her cheeks. "I'm talking about the lake," she chided him.

"Oh. The lake. My bad." He sent her what he hoped was a bashful grin. Some of Andrew's charm with the ladies must have rubbed off on him.

Holden thought it a good sign when Kayleigh slapped him lightly on the arm.

"Tell me about your family," Holden said.

Kayleigh raised one shoulder. "Not much to tell. I'm an only child."

"No cousins?"

"I have two cousins, both boys. We rarely see each other. We used to spend a couple of weeks each summer camping with my grandparents. Since we've become adults, it's hard to get together."

"Are you grandparents still living?"

Kayleigh turned to face him. "Do you really want to know?"

"Sure." Holden wanted to know everything. What kind of food she liked. Favorite movies, best childhood memory. All of it. Where did her red hair come from?

Kayleigh pulled in a breath and exhaled. "Granny and Gramps used to take my cousins and me camping for two weeks every summer."

"What was your favorite place?"

Kayleigh faced toward the lake. "We did a lot of camping in New York State. But I think my favorite summer was when we drove down the coast in their motor home. We stayed for four days in North Carolina in the Outer Banks. It was amazing."

"Do you still enjoy camping?"

"I miss it. Haven't been since Gramps died a few years ago."

"I'm sorry." Holden laid a hand on Kayleigh's arm, lying on the lounger armrest. He was heartened when she didn't pull away. "My grandma died last year. Grandfather retired from our family business and moved to Florida."

Kayleigh huffed out a laugh. "Family business? You make it sound like a mom-and-pop convenience store instead of the behemoth real estate development company."

Holden put a hand on his chest in mock outrage. "Miss Kayleigh, have you been Googling my family enterprise?"

She sent him a baleful glance. "You did give me access to your computer, you know. I'm sorry if you neglected to password protect your secret documents."

Holden inwardly cringed. How much snooping had Kayleigh done into his finances? Had she seen the legal documents about his former business partner, David? His medical records were also stored on his computer. He shouldn't have trusted her. Look what happened the last time he trusted someone.

Time to shut this conversation down. Holden made a move to stand. "I better make sure Andrew hasn't broken any dishes. You should go home." His voice sounded cold. He instantly regretted his words when Kayleigh shot to her feet.

Mr. Cranky Pants was back. Kayleigh's shoulders drooped as she called Luna and Rocky to her. The gate snapped closed behind her. Back in the Donaldson's yard, she straightened. Stupid man. She thought they'd shared a moment. Apparently, she was wrong.

Luna and Rocky cocked their heads, as if waiting to see what Kayleigh would do.

"You two stay out here for a moment. I'm gonna grab my guitar."

The evening sky was beginning to darken when Kayleigh returned to the back deck. She sat on the steps leading from the deck to the expanse of green lawn. A slight breeze blew from the lake, bringing the scent of natural gas and rotten eggs. Tourists often complained about the smell, but native New Yorkers accepted the lake's unique odor.

The guitar strings hummed under Kayleigh's fingers. Tonight was not a night for creating a new song or working on an existing one. Playing well-known tunes helped empty her mind. She started with *Yesterday* by Paul McCartney and moved into *Killing Me Softly*.

Her stress and anger floated away as she strummed. Tears filled her eyes as she played the last notes of the song.

"I'm a hot mess," she whispered.

Kayleigh was in serious 'like' with Holden. Despite his prickly exterior, there was a vulnerable man inside. Like one of the marshmallows she and her cousins used to roast in the campfire—black and crispy on the outside and gooey mush when she took a bite. Exactly as Jenna had said.

"Forget it, girlfriend." No way did Holden feel anything for her, except maybe contempt.

The dog's ears peaked at the sound of the gate

opening and closing. Kayleigh's pulse accelerated at the sight of a man making his way through the hedge.

Had Holden come to apologize for his abruptness? Nope, not Holden. The man didn't carry a cane.

"Over here, Andrew," Kayleigh called.

She watched his tall form approach and couldn't help wish it was his brother.

"I heard you playing," Andrew said.

Kayleigh's face burned. Sound carried too well in the thick evening air.

"You're good." Andrew dropped onto the step next to her and nudged her with his knee.

Kayleigh bent her face over her guitar. "Thanks."

"I was hoping you'd still be at Holden's when I finished cleaning up."

If only she was attracted to Andrew. But no, she had to like the guy with the personality of a piranha.

"Yeah, Holden told me to go home."

Andrew shifted beside her. "I apologize on behalf of my brother. He can be a bit abrupt sometimes."

"Ya think?"

The moon glinted off Andrew's teeth as he smiled. "He didn't used to be like that. BC, before cancer, he actually had fun."

"Somehow I can't quite picture that."

"He's had a tough six months. I don't know if he told you about his friend David?"

"No. What about him?" Holden had a friend? Hard to imagine.

Andrew inhaled and blew out the breath. "Holden and David were almost as close as Holden and me. Like brother-close. David was on the board of Holden Holdings. One day, our CFO alerted Holden that a large amount of money had been wired out of our operating account. That same day, David disappeared."

"Wow. Where did he go? And did he take the money?"

"Our forensic accountant traced the money. To make a long story short, David is now being held on a million-dollar bail. Shortly after the theft, Holden was diagnosed with sarcoma. The doctors removed a tumor, and Holden went through six weeks of chemo, followed by radiation."

Kayleigh picked at one of the callouses on her ring finger. "You think that's why the personality change?"

"One hundred percent."

"Your mom said something about not sure how long we all have to live. I think she was hinting that Holden might die young."

Andrew's voice lowered. "Our doctor said if his scans are clear for the next five years, he could live a long life." Andrew shrugged. "But what Mom said was true. None of us know when we'll die. The number of our days is known only by God."

"That's what my Granny says."

"Holden seems to think he is unattractive to the opposite sex because he's 'broken.'"

Kayleigh chuckled. "Unattractive? Uh, no. Have you or he looked in the mirror lately?"

It was Andrew's turn to laugh. "My brother is incredibly stubborn. He doesn't think I know this, but Holden thinks he's sterile because of the radiation. But Doc Sanford says unless he's willing to have a certain test, he'll never know."

"So he *could* reproduce," Kayleigh said.

Andrew shrugged again. "He could. Who knows?"

Kayleigh strummed a chord on her guitar. She'd be bitter, too if her best friend betrayed her and stole a bunch of money.

Andrew slapped his hands on his thighs and got to his feet. "I better get back. I don't want to explain to my brother where I was. He's jealous."

Kayleigh laughed. "Of me? With you?"

"Yup. I hope you'll show him some grace. He likes you, ya know."

"Hah. Not likely. He's like, hot and cold all within the space of a nanosecond."

Andrew was already striding toward the hedge separating the two properties. "Grace," he called over his shoulder.

JANE DALY

Chapter 27

"Holden, you're an idiot," Andrew said, stepping into Holden's bedroom.

"I'm trying to sleep, Drew."

Holden cringed as his brother sat on the edge of the king-sized bed. What torment did his brother have to inflict?

"I was next door, talking to Kayleigh."

"Good for you. Now go away." Holden laid an arm across his eyes.

"Sometimes I wonder how we're twins."

"Me too. So?"

Holden heard Andrews deep sigh. "Did cancer make you blind, deaf, and dumb?"

Holden bristled. "No, but it left me crippled. In case you hadn't noticed." He was unable to keep the bitterness from his voice.

"That's temporary. Your idiotness seems to be permanent."

"That isn't a word."

"Okay, your stupidity seems to be permanent."

"What are you talking about?" Andrew was getting on Holden's last nerve. "Say what you have to say and get out of my bedroom."

The bed shifted as Andrew stood. Holden didn't need to open his eyes to know Andrew stared down at him.

Andrew's voice, so like his own, sounded loud in Holden's ears. "You. Kayleigh. If you don't act on your feelings, and soon, she'll be gone, and you'll be alone. Again."

Andrew strode from the room.

Alone. Like he preferred. No one to pester him. No one to ask him questions he didn't want to answer. No one to cool his fever, change his sweaty sheets, and make him chicken and dumplings.

No feisty redhead to challenge him and make him laugh.

Holden fell asleep and woke coughing and gasping for breath. His head ached and his lungs felt like they were on fire. He reached for his phone on the nightstand and knocked it onto the floor. Groaning, he leaned over to pick it up and was hit with another coughing fit.

Holden fell back against the pillow, drained. Glancing over at the wing chair, he pictured Kayleigh sleeping there when he first became ill.

He should have been satisfied he'd shoved her away. Once she found out his secret, she'd move on to someone whole.

Why did that thought scare him to his core? He could die here alone in this huge, empty house and his body wouldn't be discovered for days. Andrew would go back to his fishing business, Mom and Dad were busy with their lives, and Jenna too.

Holden sank into self-pity.

Isn't that what you wanted? To be left alone?

Not anymore.

Holden curled on his side as another coughing spell snatched his breath.

A warm hand touched his bare shoulder. "What can I do to help?"

Disappointed that it was Andrew and not Kayleigh, he pointed to his phone lying face down on the Berber carpet.

"Text the doc and tell him to come ASAP," Holden said.

"H, it's four a.m."

"That's why we pay him the big bucks. To come when we call."

Holden watched his brother use his face to unlock Holden's phone. Andrew's fingers tapped on the screen.

"Okay. Done. Now what can I get you?"

"Ice cold water," Holden said, squeezing the words out before coughing again.

A few minutes later, Andrew appeared carrying a sweating bottle of Fiji spring water. Holden pulled himself to a sitting position and took the water. He downed half of it and handed the bottle back to his brother.

"Thanks. I can't stop coughing."

"Do you have a thermometer somewhere? You're burning up."

"I don't know. Maybe. But you could grab some ibuprofen from my bathroom."

Holden squeezed his eyes shut when Andrew turned on the bathroom light.

"Here." Andrew shook a bottle of pills in Holden's direction.

Holden moaned. Even that small noise was like hammers behind his eyes. "Hand me two," he said, holding open his palm. He downed the pills with the rest of the water.

"Dude, you're really sick."

"Thank you, Captain Obvious."

He felt rather than saw Andrew's grin. "I see you haven't lost your charming personality."

Holden heard the wing chair squeak as Andrew sat.

"Holden, if you get me sick, I'll kill you."

"No need. I'm dying." Or at least he felt like he was.

"No, you're not. You're going to live a ridiculously long life surrounded by six kids and fifteen grandkids."

"If only."

"H, if you were going to die, I'd know it. Remember, I'm the one who told you to get that pain in your hip looked at. I *knew* it was serious. If you hadn't waited so long ..." Andrew's voice trailed off.

Andrew was right. Holden had put off going calling Doc Sanders, terrified of what it might be. His fears were confirmed when it turned out to be cancer.

Holden sucked in a shallow breath, held it, and let his breath out slowly. When he didn't immediately cough, he asked, "I need your help."

"With Kayleigh." It wasn't a question.

"Yeah."

Holden cracked open his eyelids to see Andrew watching him with a grin. "Finally."

After Andrew disappeared into the bushes, Kayleigh called in the dogs and closed the back door.

She found her laptop on the living room coffee table.

Searching through the Trash folder, she pulled up the email from Oliver Young and reread it. Before she could change her mind, Kayleigh sent him a response.

"Thank you for reaching out. I am available," Kayleigh paused. No reason to let him think she was always available.

"I'm available afternoons from three o'clock to five o'clock for a Zoom call."

She held her breath and pressed Send. If this Oliver Young person asked for money, she'd tell him to pound sand. What was it Granny used to say? Once bitten twice shy. Or something like that.

Speaking of Granny, Kayleigh set the laptop down and went to the kitchen for the lottery tickets Granny had sent. Two tickets with some random numbers Granny had picked. The drawing would be in a few days.

"Ha, like I'm going to win anything." Her voice echoed against the twelve-foot ceiling. She tossed the tickets on the coffee table and retrieved her guitar.

She spent the next two hours working on song lyrics and jotting down some potential chords to accompany the words.

Exhaustion pulled her upstairs to her bedroom. She put on her pajamas and sank onto the feather-soft mattress. It had been a long day. Dinner with the twins, bantering with them over a shared meal, being dismissed by Mr. Cranky, and Andrew asking her to extend grace to his brother.

Grace was a concept Kayleigh was familiar with. Granny's unflappable faith in God had trickled down to Kayleigh's parents and to her. How many times had

Granny insisted she show grace when girls at school had teased her?

Kill them with kindness, Granny had told her.

Could she show grace to Gary Golden? *Nope, not there yet.*

But for Holden, she'd work on it. Kayleigh couldn't imagine having a friend betray her and steal money. Plus, a cancer diagnosis.

Okay, God, I'll be nice to Mr. Cranky Pants.

Kayleigh woke the next morning with new resolve. A quick check of her email left her disappointed that Oliver Young hadn't responded. Fine. He was probably busy.

Grace.

She fed the dogs and let them out to do their morning business while she got ready. Kayleigh took special care to brush her hair and pull it low on her neck, securing it with a clip. A bit of brown mascara made her blue eyes pop. A hint of coral lip gloss and she was ready to face whatever grace she needed to show Holden.

Luna and Rocky bounded next to her, pushing their way into Holden's yard the minute she opened the gate. Kayleigh spied Holden and Andrew sitting at one of the patio tables, a mug of steaming coffee in front of each.

"Did you save any for me?" she asked, smiling and inhaling the scent.

"Of course." Andrew sprang up from his seat and motioned for Kayleigh to take his seat. "I'll run in and grab you a cup. Cream?"

Kayleigh shook her head. "Just black, please."

Holden sipped his coffee, holding her gaze over the rim of the mug. "You're up and around early."

Kayleigh raised one shoulder. "I thought you might have something for me to do."

"I thought you might be here to have Andrew take you for a boat ride before he leaves." Holden covered his mouth as his body shook with a teeth-rattling cough.

"You should have that looked at," Kayleigh said, her face scrunching in alarm. "You sound awful."

Holden took several small sips of coffee. "Gee, thanks."

"I'm serious. You sound like you're about to cough up a lung."

Holden let out a shallow breath. "Doc Sanford is coming over soon."

He seemed like he wanted to say more but pressed his lips together instead.

Andrew stepped onto the deck with a white mug. "Here's your coffee, ma'am." He set the mug on the table with a slight bow. Kayleigh smiled up at him. "Thank you, kind sir."

Andrew sat next to Holden. Kayleigh marveled again at their identical looks. The only difference was Holden's sunken cheeks held the evidence of his illness.

"I'm going to finish my coffee and take off. I have clients waiting this afternoon," Andrew said.

Holden nodded. "Thanks for being here, Drew."

Andrew drained his mug and stood. "Let me know what the doc says."

Kayleigh noted the beads of sweat forming on Holden's forehead. His face was pale and ashen. "Do you have a fever?"

Holden covered his mouth as a fit of coughing shook his frame. "Probably," he gasped.

Kayleigh watched with concern as Holden struggled to breathe. Two thoughts warred within her. One, that Holden's cancer had returned and settled into his lungs. And two, that he was contagious, and she would get sick.

Grace.

"Can I get you anything?" Kayleigh asked, pushing herself to the edge of the chair.

"No. Doc Sanford should be here soon."

Andrew stepped through the back door clutching an overnight bag. "Now that Kayleigh's here, I'm gonna go. She can listen for the doorbell."

Kayleigh nodded.

Andrew patted Holden on the shoulder. "Be sure to text me what Doc says."

Holden's voice was tight. "I will."

With a nod in Kayleigh's direction, Andrew strode down the sloping yard and disappeared into the hedge near the lake's edge.

"I wish I had siblings," she commented.

With a wry smile, Holden said, "Sometimes, I wish I didn't."

Kayleigh shot him a glare. "He cares about you, and he's worried."

Holden opened his mouth to speak but was interrupted by the chiming of the doorbell.

Kayleigh shot to her feet. "I'll get that."

She opened the massive wood front door to welcome Dr. Sanford.

"Hello, young lady," Dr. Sanford said, stepping into the house. "I didn't expect to see you here again."

Kayleigh grasped the doctor's arm. "I'm worried about him. His cough sounds awful, and I think the fever has come back."

Dr. Sanford laid a hand over Kayleigh's. "That's why I'm here. We'll figure out what's going on."

Kayleigh trailed him as he made his way through the living room and the sunroom to step outside.

Before Holden could greet his doctor, another coughing spell grabbed him. When he was finished, he took a sip of lukewarm coffee to try to soothe the fire in his throat.

Dr. Sanford pulled a chair close and studied him. "That cough sounds brutal. Let's get your temp."

He pulled a forehead thermometer from his black bag and ran it over Holden's forehead.

"Do you want me to leave?" Kayleigh asked. Her face was filled with worry.

"You can stay." Holden hated the rasp in his voice.

Dr. Sanford studied the thermometer reading with a frown. "One hundred point five. Have you had an ibuprofen or aspirin? Anything?"

Holden nodded and held up two fingers.

"How long ago?" Dr. Sanford asked, pulling out his stethoscope.

Holden shrugged. When did Andrew give him the tablets? "Four or five a.m."

"Lift your shirt and lean forward," Doc said, standing and walking around behind him.

Holden smothered a smile when Kayleigh averted her gaze from his bare torso.

He breathed in and out at Doc's instructions. His

chest burned with the urge to cough. "I feel like an elephant is sitting on my chest." Just saying those few words brought on more hacking.

Dr. Sanford pressed Holden's neck, probing until Holden coughed again.

"Your glands are swollen." Doc pulled the stethoscope from around his neck and returned to his chair. "I'm going to take some blood."

"You can do that?" Kayleigh asked.

Doc sent her a wink. "You'd be amazed at what I can do."

Holden rolled his eyes. First his brother, and now Dr. Sanford was flirting with Kayleigh. Holden couldn't help but notice how pretty she was in the bright morning sunlight. Flecks of gold glinted in her red hair. His eyes were drawn to the shiny coral color on her full lips. What would it be like to kiss her? Would she welcome his kiss, or shove him away? With his luck, he'd start coughing and gross her out.

"Are you sure you don't want me to leave?" Kayleigh asked as Doc pulled a syringe and two vials from his bag.

"You won't pass out will you—at the sight of blood?" Doc asked, laying a towel on the table.

Kayleigh shook her head.

Holden waited for Doc to get set up to draw his blood. His stomach roiled. What would his labs show? Had cancer decided to march from his hip to his chest like an invading army?

Holden woke every morning, worrying that a few intrepid cancer cells waited for the opportunity to strike in a new part of his body.

After a sharp pinch, Holden watched bright red

blood pour into the glass vials. A song from church ran a loop through his brain. *There's power in the blood.*

Holden focused on the doctor's hands as he replaced one full container with an empty one. More blood. "What do you think, Doc? Am I going to die?"

Doc completed his ministrations and loosened the tourniquet. "We're all going to die, son."

Holden's mouth filled with questions that remained unasked.

As if sensing his anxiety, Dr. Sanford put his tools away and laid a hand on Holden's arm. "You may have walking pneumonia," he said. "Or mono. Today is not your day to die, Holden."

Holden shot a glance in Kayleigh's direction. "Isn't mono called 'the kissing disease'?"

Doc laughed. "Yes, it is. It's highly contagious." Doc looked from Holden to Kayleigh. "I advise against any kissing activity until I get the results from your blood test back from the lab."

Kayleigh's face blazed with color.

Holden coughed. "Not to worry, Doc."

Dr. Sanford addressed Kayleigh. "You should quarantine yourself for at least a week. If Holden, here, has mono, you need to let me know right away if you start to feel ill." Doc turned back to Holden. "And let your family know, too, if the test comes back positive."

Holden took another sip of his coffee while Doc dug around in his bag.

"I'm going to swab your throat to rule out strep."

At Doc's instructions, Holden opened his mouth. His gag reflex kicked in, setting off another bout of coughing. When he was done, Doc continued to swab Holden's raw throat.

"All finished," Doc said, sliding the instrument of torture back into its sleeve.

Kayleigh jumped to her feet, swiping at her eyes. "I'll get you something cold to drink."

Holden wiped his own eyes, watering from gagging and coughing.

Doc tilted his head toward Kayleigh's retreating back. "You've got a good one, there, Holden."

Holden couldn't help his loud sigh. "I don't know, Doc."

Dr. Sanford narrowed his eyes. "Holden, I've known you since you were a baby. I've watched your grow up, take over your family's business, and make your mark in the world. But you're unhappy." Doc snapped his bag closed. "Here's my unofficial medical advice. Stop stressing over your cancer coming back. I've been assured by every member of your oncology team that they got it all."

Doc stood and leaned over. Holden had to strain his neck to look up at him.

"Start living your life again. If you like that girl, I mean *woman*, let her know. She's a keeper, Holden Jeffries."

With that, Doc picked up his bag and walked into the house.

Chapter 28

Kayleigh filled a tumbler with ice and water. Before she could return outside, Dr. Sanford stepped into the kitchen.

"How are you feeling?" he asked.

"I'm feeling fine. But now, I'm worried I'm going to get sick."

Dr. Sanford laid a hand on her shoulder. "As soon as I get the lab results back, I'll let Holden know. He can pass the results on to you. If you fall ill, I'll write a prescription for you."

A bit of Kayleigh's worry melted away. "Thanks."

"In the meantime, keep an eye on our patient. Make sure he stays out of trouble."

Kayleigh chuckled. "Like I can single-handedly do that."

The doctor held her gaze for several seconds. "Miss Kayleigh, I've been around the block more than a few times. From my observation, it wouldn't take you much effort to have that man wrapped around your pinkie finger."

Kayleigh snorted. "I doubt it."

Doc quirked an eyebrow. "Get him through this bout of flu or whatever and see what happens." He winked and headed toward the front door. "You have my business card in case you start getting symptoms."

Kayleigh slowed her steps as she returned to Holden's deck. He'd moved to a lounger in the shade and reclined with his eyes closed. Rocky and Luna lay on either side of the lounger, snoozing.

"Here's your water," Kayleigh said, extending the tumbler in Holden's direction.

He opened his eyes, and their gazes locked.

"Here's your water," she repeated when he didn't reach for the tumbler. Her pulse spiked as he regarded her with those amazing blue eyes.

Their fingers touched when he raised his hand to take the water.

"Thank you."

Two simple words laced with a hundred more unspoken. Kayleigh's stomach did a barrel roll. Even feverish, coughing, and pale, Holden was the whole package. Dangerously handsome, ridiculously wealthy, and definitely single. What woman wouldn't be attracted to him?

She was, and that scared her more than the potential of catching whatever Holden had.

Kayleigh took a step back. "I should go."

"Please don't." Holden transferred the tumbler to his left hand and grasped her arm with his right. "I might need help climbing the stairs. My bed is yelling my name."

Was Holden really that weak or was this a ploy to get ... she couldn't imagine what ulterior motive Holden might have. He appeared weak and vulnerable. His hand slid from her arm and dropped to his side as his eyes closed.

"I'll help you upstairs, and then, I should probably go back to the Donaldson's."

Kayleigh helped him get up from the lounger. "Here, take my arm." She supported his weight as they shuffled into the house.

Kayleigh spoke over her shoulder to the dogs. "I'll be right back, guys."

Holden wheezed out a laugh. "You really think they can understand you?"

"You never know," Kayleigh said. They reached the foot of the stairs.

Holden pulled himself up one step at a time, using the carved wood banister for support on one side, and Kayleigh's shoulder on the other. They reached Holden's bedroom. Kayleigh guided him to his bed and helped him flop onto the pile of pillows.

"Want me to get you some ibuprofen?"

Holden nodded.

Kayleigh realized she'd left the tumbler of ice water on the patio. Yup, she would probably lose weight going up and down those stairs a hundred times a day.

"I'll be right back. Going to get your water."

Holden nodded again as a coughing fit wracked his body.

She dashed down the stairs, retrieved the water, and returned to find Holden asleep. She took the medicine from Holden's bathroom and set it on his nightstand along with the water.

Assured he was asleep, Kayleigh wandered through the upstairs rooms. In addition to Holden's bedroom and bathroom, there were two unoccupied bedrooms with a Jack and Jill bathroom connecting them. One of the bedrooms showed signs of Andrew's stay. The bed was unmade, and towels lay discarded on the bathroom floor.

"Good thing he has a housekeeper," she muttered.

She peeked in at Holden. Still sleeping. "May as well see if I need to let him know about any emails or if he left me a list."

No detailed list sat on Holden's desk. "I thought he said he'd made a list." She shrugged.

Kayleigh opened his laptop and scrolled through his emails, deleting the ads for male enhancements and vitamin supplements.

One email grabbed her attention with its red 'priority' flag. She debated only a minute before clicking on it.

"Dear Son," it began.

Holden woke in a hot sweat. He'd been dreaming he was walking barefoot across a windy desert. Voices called him from behind one of the sandy dunes, but when he climbed to the top, he slid down again.

His eyes focused on the bottle of ibuprofen. Had he taken any before falling asleep? He couldn't remember. He tried to call for Kayleigh, but his voice didn't make it past the tightness in his throat.

The chemo and radiation he'd endured wasn't as bad as how he felt at this moment. What if he died here, alone? How long until someone found his stiff body?

In the back of his mind, Doc's advice stung like a thousand mental paper cuts.

Tell her how you feel, Doc had said. Or something like that. How did he feel about Kayleigh? Was his sickness causing her to feel sorry for him?

Holden sank into self-pity as he considered Kayleigh's motivation for caring for him. How could she possibly be attracted to someone crippled, angry, and now deathly ill.

Tears formed in the corners of his eyes and dripped onto his pillow. Maybe Kayleigh would write a country song about nursing a dying man.

The next time she came into his room, he'd tell her to go away. He'd rather die than have anyone, especially her, see him like this.

***

Kayleigh sat back in Holden's ergonomic leather desk chair. What she'd read took several minutes for her to process.

She shouldn't have read the email from Holden's dad. Now she was stuck with the knowledge he'd been replaced. She reread the email, wondering at the implications. How would Holden react?

Dear Son, Due to recent events—David's embezzlement, your ongoing health battles, and the hit to the company's bottom line—the board held a meeting with a 'no confidence' vote. Rather than seeing Morehouse assume the position of president of the board, I have decided to step in.

This is only temporary until you are back on your feet. I am sorry to do this via email, but this needs to go into the official board meeting minutes.

Let's talk soon. Love, Dad.

How would Holden react when he read this? Not well, Kayleigh assumed.

She pushed herself up and closed the laptop with a sigh. Time to check on the patient.

Holden lay on his side. Why was it that even the

strongest man looked vulnerable curled into a fetal position? She padded out of the bedroom and down the stairs. When she reached the bottom, Holden's housekeeper, Tara, was stepping through the front door.

"Wait," Kayleigh said, holding her hand in a 'stop' position. "You may want to skip the cleaning today. Holden is sick and may be contagious. And me too."

Tara froze. Her mouth formed an O. "Okay. Um." She scratched her head. "What's wrong with him?"

"I'm waiting to hear from the doctor," Kayleigh said with a shrug. "But he said I need to quarantine myself until he gets Holden's test results back."

Tara took a step back. "Thanks for telling me. I guess I'll go."

Poor woman looked like she might throw up. "I'm sorry," Kayleigh said. "But I'd feel terrible if you caught whatever Holden has."

Tara bobbed her head as she retreated. With a final wave, she hopped in her car, tires spinning on the decomposed granite driveway as she sped down the driveway.

Kayleigh watched until Tara's taillights disappeared around a bend.

"I feel terrible," she said, "scaring her like that."

Kayleigh gathered Luna and Rocky and returned to the Donaldson's. She'd tossed the pups a chewy treat and stood in the kitchen. What to do? Should she take some of her things to Holden's in case he needed something in the middle of the night?

Her phone rang, and Sandra's face filled the screen—a FaceTime call.

"Hi, Kayleigh. How is everything? How are my babies?"

Kayleigh forced her lips into a smile. "It's going great!"

"Let me see my babies," Sandra said.

Kayleigh pointed the phone to where Rocky and Luna sat on their beds, chomping on their rawhide bones.

Sandra's voice rose the way people do when they talk to babies and pets. "There are my sweet doggies. Do you miss Mom? I miss you both so much."

Good thing Sandra couldn't see Kayleigh's eye roll.

Luna and Rocky couldn't have cared less that their 'Mom' was gushing over them.

Kayleigh turned the phone around. "How's your trip?"

Sandra's face formed a frown. "We've decided to cut our trip short. Robert has a work emergency, and we'll be returning at the end of the week."

Kayleigh felt her chest tighten. The end of the week? What if Holden wasn't well? What if she got what he had and couldn't get out of bed? Would the Donaldsons kick her to the curb?

"I'm sorry to hear that." Kayleigh managed to force the words over the lump in her throat.

"Yes, I'm sorry too. But don't worry, I'll still pay you for the four weeks we promised."

That was the least of Kayleigh's worries. "That's kind of you."

Sandra's voice was full of cheer. "Okay, then, we'll see you soon. Thank you for taking care of Rocky and Luna. Bye bye."

Sandra disconnected. Kayleigh sank onto one of the kitchen chairs and stared glumly at the dogs. "That stinks." The dogs thumped their tails in agreement.

JANE DALY

Chapter 29

"Well, guys, I guess I better head back next door. Maybe the doctor will show up with test results."

The dogs scrambled to their feet and headed to the back door, pressing their noses against the glass. Kayleigh let them out, watching them frolic and roll on the soft grass. Leaving the door open, she retrieved her guitar and notebook.

Chewing her lip, she contemplated what she might need if her stay at Holden's extended into the evening hours.

"Well, it's just next door," she said, hefting her guitar case.

Luna and Rocky willingly followed her through the bushes and into Holden's backyard. Humidity pressed on her, instantly bringing sweat to her forehead. With only a moment's hesitation, she let the pups into Holden's house.

"Stay here," she commanded. Such well-behaved dogs. They sniffed the furniture, the floor, and plopped onto the area rug in front of the stone fireplace in the living room.

"Good dogs."

Kayleigh propped her guitar case against the sofa

and set her notebook on the coffee table.

"Drat. I forgot my laptop." With a backward glance toward the pups, she hustled back to the Donaldson's for her laptop. When she returned, she was relieved to see them lying in the same spot.

She set her laptop next to the notebook and went upstairs to look in on Holden. He lay on his back with one arm slung across his head.

His eyes opened when she tiptoed into the room.

"You're here," he whispered. "I'm not dreaming, am I?"

Holden's eyes were glazed with fever. Dark stubble covered his sunken cheeks.

"Can I get you anything?" Ice in the tumbler of water had melted, leaving condensation on the sides. The bottle of ibuprofen sat in the same spot where she'd left it earlier that day.

Holden pushed himself up on his elbows. "Water."

Kayleigh moved to his bedside and used a tissue to wipe down the tumbler. "Drink a little of this. I'll get some fresh ice. Did you take any of these?" she asked, shaking the pill bottle.

"No."

Kayleigh poured two tablets into her hand. Holden took them and swallowed them down with some water, wincing.

"Did you take your antibiotics today?"

"I can't remember." Holden sank back as if barely able to stay upright.

Kayleigh chewed her lips in indecision. Before she could decide whether or not to retrieve the prescription from Holden's bathroom, the front door chimed.

"Maybe that's the doctor," she said. Holden didn't

respond.

She dashed down the stairs to the front door, relieved to see Dr. Sanford on the porch holding a grocery bag.

"Come in." She swung the door wide for him to enter.

"I have Holden's test results," he said, setting the bag on the kitchen island.

"That was fast."

"That's why they pay me the big bucks," Dr. Sanford said with a smile.

Kayleigh leaned a hip against the opposite counter. "How much does something like this cost?"

Dr. Sanford pursed his lips and regarded her with narrowed eyes. "You don't want to know."

It was probably best she didn't know. Having a personal physician at your beck and call was so far out of her reach she'd never begin to imagine.

Still, her curiosity got the better of her. "Like, six figures?"

Doc chuckled. "Not quite. Let's just say a high five figures and leave it at that."

Kayleigh contemplated his answer. So not over a hundred thousand, but likely a ton of money per year to get personal service. Must be nice.

"What's in the bag?" she asked.

"Let's start with Holden's test results. You'll be relieved to know it isn't mono. But you still need to be cautious. Wash your hands, consider wearing a mask when you're around him, at least for the next day or so."

"Okay. What's the diagnosis?"

"Strep throat." Doc reached into the grocery bag for

a white prescription sack. "I have some different antibiotics and a stronger cough suppressant. He should see an improvement in twenty-four hours. Make sure he takes them for the full ten days."

Huh. She wouldn't be here in ten days. Withe the Donaldson's return, she'd probably be back in her old bedroom at her parents' house. But Doc didn't need to know her own personal drama.

Doc dug into the bag and began to lay food on the counter. "I brought fresh lemons and honey. Squeeze some lemon juice into warm water along with the honey. That should soothe his throat."

"Sounds like my granny's home remedy."

"Exactly. Sometimes simple is better. Here's some vanilla ice cream. See if you can get Holden to eat some. I'm a little concerned about his weight loss."

"Ice cream. Got it." Kayleigh'd consumed at least a gallon of ice cream when she'd had her tonsils removed.

Doc pulled a plastic container of what appeared to be chicken soup from the bag. "Nothing like chicken soup to speed healing."

Kayleigh nodded. "I don't think he's eaten anything since the chicken and dumplings a couple days ago." She rubbed a hand across her forehead. "I've lost track of time lately."

Doc nodded sagely. "It happens."

"What do I owe you for all this?" Kayleigh waved a hand across the food spread on the island.

"Not a thing. It's all part of the concierge service."

"Wow." Before Kayleigh could say more, Luna and Rocky padded into the kitchen.

"When did Holden get dogs?" Doc asked.

Kayleigh sent him a wry grin. "They're mine. Or rather they're the Donaldson's. I'm dog sitting."

"Ah. So, you're multi-talented." He ticked off on his fingers, "Dog watcher, fill-in administrative assistant, and nurse."

"Pretty much."

"Should I add 'girlfriend' to the list?" Doc asked with a grin.

Kayleigh hesitated before answering. "Probably not. In Holden's current state of health, I doubt he's thinking romance."

Doc patted her shoulder. "You never know." Then he was back to business. "You'll let me know if you start getting sick. No charge to you if you need me to make a house call."

"I will. Thank you, Dr. Sanford."

"No, my dear. Thank *you* for taking care of one of my favorite patients."

When the doctor left, Kayleigh put the food in the refrigerator and warmed a cup of water in the microwave. She added a squeeze of lemon and a dollop of honey and carried it upstairs along with the antibiotics.

She found Holden sitting on the edge of his bed, head in his hands.

"Where have you been?" he demanded.

Holden regretted the words as soon as they left his mouth. Not only rude, his throat feel like he'd swallowed a razor blade. But his head hurt with the effort to form coherent thoughts.

"I brought you some warm lemon and honey water.

You can use it to take one of the new antibiotics Dr. Sanford brought."

"Doc was here?" Holden winced. He really needed to not talk.

"He brought these," Kayleigh shook the bottle in front of his face. Even that small sound struck like a cymbal in his head.

Holden closed his eyes against the visual and auditory stimuli. Mutely, he held out his hand and let Kayleigh place a pill in his hand. He felt her push the mug in his direction after he'd put the pill in his mouth.

The warm solution burned like crazy. But after the first sip, he felt the honey coat his raw throat.

"What's the prognosis?" he asked, his voice a whisper.

"Strep."

That explained his sore throat. What about his cough? He trusted Doc to handle whatever life threw his way regarding health. What had Doc said? Something about living a long life. Or had he dreamed it? Fever filled his head with cotton.

Holden swung his legs onto the bed and flopped against his pillow. Hopefully this new antibiotic would zap the strep throat soon.

Kayleigh grabbed for the mug before it spilled over the covers. "Try to finish this next time you wake up. Your doctor also brought some soup. I'll warm some up a little later."

Holden watched Kayleigh through half-closed eyes. "You're so pretty," he whispered. "I wish ..." what did he wish? So many things, but the words got tangled up in his brain. He wished she'd lay a cool hand on his forehead. He wished she'd see him as a whole man, not one weak and broken. That she'd feel the same way about him as he did about her. He was falling, sliding over a waterfall into a pond filled with boiling water.

"Save me, Kayleigh." He managed to choke out the words before he went under.

JANE DALY

Chapter 30

Kayleigh strained to hear what Holden was mumbling in his fever-induced state. Something about falling and she could save him. Did she hear him say he wondered if she felt the same way about him that he did about her? How *did* he feel?

Holden ran hot and cold. Falling for him would be like falling into a cactus. Unfortunately, it was too late. She was entangled in an invasive cactus, and the spines pierced her heart.

With one last look at Holden's prone form, Kayleigh returned downstairs and stood in the living room. Luna and Rocky had made themselves at home on the hearth rug. Luna cracked open her eyes when Kayleigh plopped onto the sofa, then returned to her nap with a sigh.

The leather sofa creaked as Kayleigh leaned back, pondering the email from Holden's dad. When his fever broke, Holden would be furious his board basically shoved him out. At least Mick had his son's back.

Before opening her music-writing notebook, Kayleigh pulled her laptop onto her lap. She held her breath when she saw a response from Oliver Young, the music producer. Before she could click on the email, the doorbell rang.

"Sheesh. Is Dr. Sanford bringing more food?"

Kayleigh pushed herself up from the sofa, strode to the front door, and flung it open.

Not the doctor, but a medium height man wearing jeans and a short-sleeved button up shirt. His blonde hair was cut military-short.

"Hello, beautiful."

Kayleigh mentally rolled her eyes. Who was this tool? "Can I help you?"

"Can I come in?" The guy had the audacity to put one foot on the threshold.

"Not until you tell me who you are and what you want." Kayleigh squared her shoulders and tightened her grip on the doorframe.

"I didn't know Holden had hired a guard dog." He looked ready to push past her.

Kayleigh's pulse spiked as adrenaline coursed through her veins. Who was this guy who thought he could muscle his way past her?

"Luna! Rocky! Come."

Behind her, the click of the dog's nails on the wood floor told her the dogs were dashing toward the door. They skidded to a stop next to her and started to bark.

The guy held up his hands in surrender. "Whoa, whoa. I'm here to see Holden. That's all."

"And you are?" Kayleigh asked.

With a cautious look at Luna and Rocky, the man extended his hand. "David Sommers. I'm a friend of Holden's."

"He's not feeling well. You'll have to come back later." Kayleigh attempted to close the door again, but David put a hand on the door to stop her.

"Will you tell him I was here? I'd like to talk with him."

"I'll give him the message."

"Down, Luna. Down, Rocky." The dogs continued to growl until Kayleigh shut the door. Just like the pups, the hair on the back of her neck prickled. Who was David Sommers? Was this the same David who Andrew said stole money? If Holden wasn't in a fever fog, she'd ask.

Back to the email. Kayleigh held her breath and clicked on the email.

Dear Miss McGuire,

I apologize for the delay in responding. We've been swamped here. How does tomorrow sound? I can send you a Zoom link to meet at 11:00 am Central Time.

Cordially,

Oliver Young

Kayleigh took several cleansing breaths to calm her racing pulse.

She typed a response.

"That sounds perfect. Talk to you soon."

Kayleigh stared at the email, but there was no response within a couple of minutes. She closed the laptop and went to the back door to let the dogs outside.

"I'm going to run home and get my swimsuit," she told them. As if they understood, they raced to the hedge and disappeared into their own backyard.

Holden's pool was just the right temperature. Cool enough to be a refreshing break from the heat, but not cold enough to chill her. Kayleigh swam several laps, then dog-paddled in the deep end and sat behind the waterfall.

When she was rich and famous, she'd definitely

have a house with a pool. And heated year-round, too.
She was startled out of her daydreaming by a female voice. "That looks fun."

Startled, Kayleigh gulped a mouthful of pool water. She came up sputtering and coughing.

"I'm sorry! I didn't mean to scare you." Holden's sister, Jenna walked to the pool's edge and crouched down. "Come on out and let me pound you on the back."

Kayleigh paddled to the steps and came out of the water, pushing her hair out of her eyes.

"I'm fine. You startled me, that's all." She grabbed a towel on the small table near the pool.

"I'm sorry. Andrew said I needed to see if you needed any help nursing Holden back to health."

Kayleigh blew out a breath through pursed lips. "Your timing is impeccable," she said with a smile.

"How are you doing," Jenna asked when they'd poured themselves frosty glasses of Coke Zero.

How was she doing? Kayleigh was confused at this point. She was falling, or had fallen, for a guy who was lying in bed mumbling about having her 'save' him. Her current dog-sitting position was coming to a crashing halt, and she had only a few hours to polish her songs before the Zoom call with Oliver Young.

Before Kayleigh could answer, Jenna said, "Looks like your dogs have made themselves at home." She pointed a finger at Luna and Rocky, who'd resumed their positions in front of the fireplace. "Does Holden know?"

Kayleigh returned Jenna's grin. "Nope. He's

practically incoherent with fever. But Dr. Sanford sent over some new meds. Hopefully his fever will break soon."

"Isn't Doc the best?" Jenna said. "We are blessed to have him. He was a rock during Holden's surgery and treatments. He kept our parents from completely losing it."

Kayleigh tucked her legs under her on the sofa. Jenna was super likable, unlike Holden. How had the three come out of the same body at the same time, yet be so different?

"He even brought food—ice cream, soup, and honey for your brother," Kayleigh said.

"He's worth every penny," Jenna said. "Now, tell me how you're doing."

Kayleigh chewed her lip. "Well, first of all, I feel like a ticking time bomb. Your doctor said Holden was super contagious and I should quarantine myself. Every other minute, I'm checking my throat to see if I'm getting sick." Kayleigh swallowed. "Actually, you shouldn't be here."

"I'm not worried about getting sick," Jenna said. "I have a strong immune system. And I'll stay out of Holden's room."

Kayleigh nodded. "Good. Andrew used one of the guest bedrooms, but I think the other one is clean. But the bathroom ..."

Jenna laughed. "Andrew is such a slob."

"Agreed."

"Anyway, you and Holden ..." Jenna let the rest of her sentence dangle in the space between them.

Kayleigh's sigh said it all.

"I knew it!" Jenna exclaimed.

Kayleigh sighed again and laid her head back against the cool leather. "Sometimes, I don't know if your brother loathes me or likes me."

Jenna laid a hand on Kayleigh's leg. "Oh, believe me, he likes you all right." Jenna sent her an appraising glance. "You're different. You aren't afraid to challenge him, unlike these vacuous model-types he's dated before. You're down to earth. Real. He needs you."

"Ha. He needs me like another head."

Jenna's smile was smug. "How do *you* feel about my brother? I mean, most women, especially the ones in our social circle, would run screaming of they had to play nurse to a sick man."

"Can I be honest with you?" Kayleigh asked.

Jenna grinned. "Of course. Especially if we're going to be sisters-in-law."

Kayleigh rolled her eyes. "Stop. Between you and your mom, I can see plans being made behind my back."

"Like mother, like daughter," Jenna said. "Now, spill."

Chapter 31

Holden woke in a pool of sweat. His T-shirt was soaked, and his pillow clung to the back of his head. The ache behind his eyes had decreased to a dull thud.

Glancing at the nightstand, he eyed the mug sitting there. He vaguely remembered Kayleigh bringing him something warm to drink. He pulled himself up and swallowed down the liquid, wincing as it slid down his throat.

He needed a shower, hot and stinging. But his cane wasn't within eyesight. Without it, he doubted he'd make it to the bathroom without crashing to the floor.

Holden tried calling for help, but his voice came out in a rasp. His frustration mounted until he decided he couldn't wait any longer to use the bathroom. Even if it meant crawling.

His bare feet landed squarely on the carpet. So far so good. Until a fit of coughing overtook him.

"You're awake." Kayleigh's voice was a balm to his frustration. "Did your fever break?"

Holden looked over his shoulder to see Kayleigh approaching the bed and Jenna standing in the doorway, her forehead crinkled in concern.

"I think so. Can you help me to the bathroom? Or at least find my cane?"

"Of course." Kayleigh held out an arm.

Holden grasped her arm and pulled himself to his feet. He wobbled and grabbed onto the headboard until the wave of dizziness passed.

Leaning heavily on her arm, Holden limped to the bathroom. "Thanks. I'm going to shower."

"Are you sure that's wise?" Kayleigh asked.

"If you hear a crash, call 9-1-1," he said with the ghost of a smile.

Jenna chuckled. "Don't worry, H. Neither of us want to see you lying naked on the shower floor."

"What are you doing here, anyway?" Holden asked.

"Mom and Dad flew to Florida to check on Grandpa. They asked me to check on you. But I see Kayleigh has been taking good care of you."

Holden watched with interest as Kayleigh and Jenna exchanged a glance. Kayleigh narrowed her eyes.

Kayleigh pulled herself away from him. "I'll change your sheets while you're showering and warm up some of the soup your doctor brought."

Holden processed her words through the wisps of brain fog still lingering in his head. "Doc was here?"

"He said you have strep throat. He brought some more antibiotics. You don't remember?"

Holden shook his head and immediately regretted it. Twin ice picks jabbed behind his eyes. Maybe he'd feel better once he washed the sweat clinging to his body.

"Where's Tara?" His housekeeper should be keeping up with bedding and stuff.

"I told her not to come while you're still contagious," Kayleigh said.

"You had no right—" Holden began, but a fit of coughing doubled him over. He stumbled into the bathroom and brace himself against the counter.

Jenna's voice carried across the room as he swung the door closed.

"Don't be a donkey's hind-end," Jenna said.

"See? He hates me," Kayleigh said when Holden slammed the bathroom door.

Jenna walked toward the bed and pulled back the covers. "Let me help you with this."

They worked together removing the sheets.

"I'll grab a clean set from the linen closet," Jenna said, carrying the soiled sheets to the hall.

Kayleigh gathered up the empty mug and tumbler from Holden's end table and carried them downstairs to the kitchen. She poured some chicken soup into a microwave-proof bowl and zapped it for two minutes.

By the time she returned upstairs, Jenna was half-finished with making the bed.

"No bodily crashes from the bathroom yet," Jenna said with a smile.

"That's a relief," Kayleigh said. She set the warmed soup on Holden's dresser. "Let me help you finish. And wash your hands when we're done. I'd feel terrible if you got sick."

Jenna grabbed the blanket and slung it over the clean sheets. "Don't worry about me. You're the one who's been breathing my brother's air."

"True."

Together they made short work of making the bed. Kayleigh heard the water turn off in the bathroom. She looked at Jenna, trying to decide if they should wait until he came out of the bathroom or return downstairs.

Before she could ask Jenna, the bathroom door opened and Holden appeared holding a towel around his waist. Kayleigh stifled a gasp at the thinness of his legs and torso. The man couldn't afford to lose any more weight. His legs looked like uncooked spaghetti.

"Put on some clothes, H," Jenna said.

Kayleigh couldn't agree more. Even thin as he was, the man was incredible. Dark stubble covered his cheeks, evidence of his few days in bed.

"I will as soon as you ladies leave my bedroom."

Kayleigh dashed to the door, followed by Jenna.

"Let's go downstairs and finish our conversation," Jenna said, pulling the door closed behind her.

"One moment," Kayleigh said. She put her mouth up to the bedroom door. "I put a bowl of soup on your dresser. And a spoon."

Holden's reply was a grunt. Good enough.

Jenna started to giggle. "Sometimes I wonder if one of us is adopted," she said, giggling harder.

Kayleigh joined in and they laughed until their sides hurt.

The door was flung open. Holden stood with a scowl on his face. "What's so funny?"

Kayleigh and Jenna exchanged a glance and dissolved into giggles again.

Chapter 32

"I'll make us some lunch," Jenna said they reached the bottom of the stairs.

"I'll help." Kayleigh followed Holden's sister into the kitchen, watching as Jenna dug through Holden's fridge.

"There's PB&J. Looks like a lot of food in the fridge will have to be tossed."

"PB&J sounds good. I'm starved." Kayleigh leaned back against the island and watched Jenna deftly prepare two sandwiches. "Can I ask you something?"

Jenna glanced up. "Sure."

"Who is David Sommers?"

Jenna's posture stiffened. "Why do you ask?"

"He came here this morning, asking to see Holden."

Jenna's face filled with rage. "That's Holden's former business partner. The one who stole a million dollars from the company. What did he want?"

"He wanted to see Holden. I told him to go away."

"You should have told him to go to you-know-where. I doubt Holden would want to see him. How did he get out of jail?"

Kayleigh shrugged. "No idea." Kayleigh chewed her lip. "There's something else."

Jenna put the sandwiches on two plates. "Let's go into the dining room and eat first. I need sustenance."

The two women sat across from each other. Kayleigh compared Holden's and Andrews' dark hair and blue eyes with Jenna's light hair and eyes. So different and yet so connected. She'd never heard of a multiple birth like theirs.

After they'd eaten half of their sandwiches, Jenna said, "What else did you want to ask me?"

Would it be betraying Holden if she brought up the email from their dad? Without second-guessing herself, Kayleigh plunged in. "Your dad sent an email to Holden."

Jenna made a rolling motion with her hand, telling Kayleigh to speed it up.

Kayleigh sucked in a breath. "The board voted Holden out. Your dad had to step in to keep one of the members from taking over." Her nerves twinged, waiting for Jenna to respond.

Jenna set her partially eaten sandwich half on the plate and wiped her hands on a napkin. "You know this, how?"

"I read the email." Kayleigh held her breath while Jenna processed the information.

"I don't know whether to be impressed or ticked off."

Kayleigh wouldn't blame Jenna if she pointed to the door and told Kayleigh to get out. It was a serious invasion of their family's privacy. Once again, her nosiness got her into trouble.

Kayleigh's words came out in a rush. "I know, I'm sorry. But Holden had asked me to take care of his business. I went through his email and deleted a bunch of spam, and the email from your dad looked important." She inhaled and opened her mouth to say more, but Jenna put out a hand.

"Don't apologize. What's done is done. I'll talk to Holden. He will not be happy about the board. But I'll try to keep you out of it."

Kayleigh's shoulders sagged with relief. "Thanks."

The corners of Jenna's mouth tipped up. "In the meantime, what do I have to do to get you and my brother together?"

"A miracle."

Holden polished off the last of the chicken soup while sitting in the wing chair and looking through the texts that clogged his phone while he'd been asleep.

Dad: Check your email

Mom: I'm sending Jenna over to check on you. Text me and let me know how you're feeling

Andrew: How are you and your nurse getting along? This was followed by a kissing emoji.

Holden deleted the text.

Down the list he went, responding to texts until he froze.

David: Need to talk to you

Holden's blood pressure rose.

Holden: Anything you have to say can be said to my attorney.

There, that should do it. He had no interest in talking to or seeing his former friend. David had stabbed him in the back, pulled out the knife, and plunged it in again. He was probably trying to get Holden Holdings and Holden to drop the embezzlement charges.

That wasn't going to happen. David had probably used some of the funds he'd stolen to post bond. Otherwise, David wouldn't have had access to his cell phone. Holden hoped his former friend would get the most severe penalty allowed by New York law. Seven years and a hefty fine wouldn't be stringent enough.

Holden doubted his company would ever retrieve the money David had taken. How would he pay it back if he was in prison?

It wasn't about the money. Not really. The company would absorb the loss and move on. It was the principle. David's betrayal of their friendship was the unforgivable sin.

Tired of being confined to his room and bed, Holden pushed himself to his feet and made his way to the top of the stairs. Voices from the dining room drifted up. Jenna and Kayleigh. Straining to listen, he took one step at a time and descended the staircase.

Holden paused at the bottom step, realizing he'd made a mistake in thinking he was well enough to be up and around. His chest ached and the urge to cough tickled his throat. But he wanted to hear the girls' conversation.

"I think you two make a cute couple," Jenna said.

"Sure. Like oil and vinegar." Kayleigh sounded annoyed.

"Oil and vinegar make a great salad dressing. You have to shake them together to get a delicious outcome."

"Yeah, I'd like to shake your brother by the neck."

Ouch.

Jenna laughed. "So would I. But seriously, he does

like you."

There was a pause before Kayleigh responded. What was she thinking? He'd love to know what went on her head. Holden feared he'd lost his heart to a woman who thought he was a complete tool.

"He has a funny way of showing it."

Some movement of his must have alerted them to his presence. The sound of chairs scraping back had him moving from his position at the bottom of the stairs and into the living room.

Jenna and Kayleigh stood in the doorway to the dining room, mouths open.

"What are you doing out of bed?" Jenna demanded.

Holden glanced from his sister to Kayleigh and over to where Luna and Rocky lay in front of the hearth.

"Why are those dogs in my house?"

JANE DALY

Chapter 33

As if Luna and Rocky knew they were the object of Holden's ire, they scrambled to their feet and dashed to the back door.

Kayleigh let them out and turned back to Holden. "Why are you up? You should be lying down."

Holden frowned. "I'm tired of being in bed." He swooned and looked ready to pass out.

She rushed to him and grabbed his arm. "Sit down on the sofa." She practically pushed him down.

Holden grunted. A coughing spell had him bent over his thighs.

"I'm going to get you some water," Jenna said.

Kayleigh sank onto the couch next to Holden. "Seriously, you aren't totally well yet."

She watched Holden struggle to breathe. When he'd stopped coughing, he laid his head back.

"When do I take more antibiotics?" he asked.

Kayleigh glanced at the gold anniversary clock high up on the mantle. "Now." She stood and dashed upstairs to retrieve the prescription. She picked up Holden's empty soup bowl and carried both downstairs to the kitchen.

She found Jenna in the living room, coaxing Holden

to down a glass of ice water. Kayleigh tipped one capsule from the prescription bottle and held it out for Holden to take.

His fingers were cool on the palm of her hand, a change from the heat that had radiated off his body under the fever. If he rested and took his antibiotics as scheduled, Holden should be well by the time she had to leave the Donaldson's. And she'd be finished playing nurse to an ungrateful patient.

The thought of never seeing Holden again brought a flush of sadness. Despite everything, Kayleigh enjoyed sparring with him. What would it be like to coax Mr. Cranky back to the way he was before cancer turned him into a grump?

"I'm going to change into my swimsuit and jump into that beautiful pool." Jenna headed for the stairs with one backward glance. She caught Kayleigh's eye and winked.

Kayleigh stared down at Holden. His head rested on the back of the sofa. "Can I get you anything?"

"I'm hungry. What is there to eat?"

"Your doctor brought ice cream. How does that sound?"

"Heavenly."

Kayleigh searched the kitchen cupboards for a mid-sized bowl and filled it with vanilla ice cream. She carried it into the living room and set it on the coffee table. Holden had straightened and held his cell phone in one hand.

Holden's blue eyes blazed when he looked up. "Did you read my email from my dad?"

Kayleigh froze. "I, uh—"

Holden shook his phone in her direction. "The

email shows it was read. By you?"

Kayleigh licked her lips. "You were, I mean ..." In a moment, her temper flared. "Calm down. You've had me go through your emails before. Why are you riled up about this one?"

Holden's voice rose to match hers. "Because it was private. You had no right."

Angry heat filled her with burning flames. "Look, Holden Jeffries, this is the last time I will be yelled at by you."

Holden grasped his cane and rose to his feet to face her. "I am not yelling. I am asking why you thought it was acceptable to read a private message from my father."

Kayleigh flung her arms out to the side. "This isn't about one email. This is about you second-guessing everything I do."

Holden took two steps toward her. They stood inches apart. Kayleigh could see the dark blue circles surrounding his blue corneas.

She dropped her arms and placed them on her hips. The air stilled, silent and thick with emotion. They held each other's gaze. Hers, flashing with anger. His, filled with an intensity Kayleigh didn't recognize.

"As a matter of fact, I quit. The Donaldson's will be back Saturday, and I'll be gone."

The expression in Holden's eyes changed to surprise. "You're leaving?"

She wouldn't be taken in by Holden's sudden vulnerability. "Yes. I'm going back to Nashville. You and your admin job can go—"

Holden grabbed her by the shoulders, shocking her into silence. He pulled her close and covered her mouth with his.

His kiss was soft yet firm and tasted of vanilla ice cream. Kayleigh's arms went around him as if they belonged to someone else. Holden pulled her closer and continued to plunder her mouth. Kayleigh heard Jenna's footsteps as she crossed the room and headed to the back door. But she was unable to pull herself away from Holden's embrace.

Hadn't she wanted this? To be held by this man and to find out if the undercurrent of emotion flowing between them was real.

It was real, all right. Kayleigh kissed Holden back with intensity that surprised herself. She ran her hands down his back, feeling his bones poking through his skin. The man needed someone to take care of him. But how could she do that if she was forced to leave the Donaldson's?

Kayleigh pulled away and her arms dropped to her sides. She and Holden faced each other.

"I should say I'm sorry. But I'm not," Holden said.

Nerves tingled in Kayleigh's hands like she'd grabbed an electronic fence. "I should go."

Holden's grasp on her shoulders loosened as she stepped back. She took one last longing look at him before dashing to the door and to the safety of the Donaldson's house.

Holden tried to follow Kayleigh, but he wasn't fast enough to catch her. "Stupid cane," he muttered, stepping onto the back porch. He caught a flash of red hair as Kayleigh ducked under the hedge and disappeared into his neighbor's yard.

Jenna called to him from the deep end of his pool. "What was that, H? You must be a lousy kisser if Kayleigh is running away already."

Holden returned her cheeky grin with a glare. "Go home, Jenna."

"Not on your life, brother. I'm staying here until you two figure things out."

Holden shook his head and returned to the house. After another reviving shower and another dose of ibuprofen and cough syrup, he was ready to face his demons.

His attraction to Kayleigh had been growing since she'd played that song for him. The one about a simple life. Bare feet and porch swings. His life was anything but simple. Running his family's real estate empire meant attending fundraising galas, uncomfortable tuxedos, and hobnobbing with people he rarely knew.

What kind of life was that for someone who wanted backyard barbecues and concerts in the park?

Holden smacked his forehead. Why had he kissed her? That had put him over the edge. He was in love with Kayleigh. But she was on a quest to break into the music business.

In Nashville.

Almost a thousand miles away.

It might as well be a million.

Holden opened his laptop and sent a response to his father's email, short and concise.

Dad,

Thank you. I appreciate you having my back. I'll work on getting healthy so I can resume my position.

He scrolled through his emails and stopped on one

from his private investigator. The subject line read 'Golden Boy.'

Holden, I located your guy in a little town in South Carolina. He's using the name Gary Goldstein. How would you like me to proceed?

Holden read and reread the email. Kayleigh had no idea he'd sent his PI to find the man who'd crushed her dreams. Would she be angry or relieved? Hard to tell with her quick temper.

He exhaled and tapped out a response.

Chapter 34

Kayleigh let Luna and Rocky in the house and pulled her phone from the pocket of her denim skirt. Granny had called while she was in the middle of kissing Holden. She'd ignored the buzzing from her pocket. Maybe it would have been better if she'd answered Granny's call instead of kissing Holden back.

What a kiss. Kayleigh rubbed her index finger across her lips, still tingling from Holden's unshaven cheeks. It wasn't *A* kiss, it was *The* kiss. One she'd never forget.

This couldn't be happening. She'd be gone in a couple of days and the chances of seeing Holden again were slim to none. She was hot dogs and hamburgers on a Weber barbecue and Holden was filet mignon in a Michelin restaurant.

Her heart would only be crushed if she admitted her desire to have a relationship with Holden. But her stomach whirled every time he pinned her with those icy blue eyes. She had every right to swell with burning anger when he snapped at her, but instead, she felt fluttery and on edge.

Kayleigh's thoughts swung back to how it felt being in his arms. Safe. Cared for. *Loved.*

How could she love someone so cranky, yet vulnerable in his illness.

She remembered a line from one of her favorite movies, *The Proposal*. 'We're just two people who never meant to fall in love.'

Yup, that pretty much summed it up. She was in love with Holden, but there was no way in God's green earth a relationship could work.

With a deep sigh, Kayleigh listened to the voice mail from Gran.

"Kayleigh, honey, don't forget to check those lottery numbers. Who knows, maybe you'll be a winner. Love, you."

She wandered to the kitchen island and pushed the two lottery tickets with one finger.

"Sure, Granny. A winner. What are the odds?"

She picked up the slips of paper with the numbers marching across in straight lines and allowed herself a moment to daydream.

What would she do if she won a million dollars? Fly to Nashville, rent a nice apartment, and pay for enough studio time to produce a record she could shop to music producers. Even if it took a year or more, there'd be enough money to tide her over.

Kayleigh created a mental list of dreams.

Buy a car

Buy a new guitar

"Sorry, Marty, but you'll still be my favorite." Marty didn't respond from his perch on the kitchen table.

Kayleigh bit her lip. There wasn't anything she was dying to buy or do. She had no desire to travel overseas. Her only desire of breaking into the music scene was slowly being overshadowed by the desire to be with Holden.

Peeling back his crusty exterior had revealed a man who would protect her, adore her, and challenge her. Could she give up Nashville for Holden Jeffries?

The Zoom call with Oliver Young went better than Kayleigh expected. Despite her nerves, she'd managed to wow the music guy.

"When can you get to Nashville," he'd asked.

Kayleigh hesitated only a moment before responding. "I can be there on Monday." The Donaldsons' latest text indicated they'd be home a day earlier than expected. Tomorrow, Kayleigh could pack up her things and ask Dad to pick her up. One night at her parents and she'd head to Nashville Sunday.

Mr. Young sent Kayleigh the address of his office in downtown Nashville. After confirming the time and adding it to her calendar, Kayleigh collapsed against the sofa and hugged herself.

"It's really happening," she said to Rocky and Luna. Kayleigh could swear the dogs grinned up at her.

She jumped when her phone rang with Granny's distinctive ring tone. *Sweet Home Alabama* sounded through the tiny speaker.

"Kayleigh, you have to go to the New York Lottery website." Granny's voice was breathless with excitement.

Kayleigh pulled her laptop onto her crossed legs. "What's going on, Granny?"

"I took a picture with my phone. I didn't know the picture would be so clear, by the way."

"What's this about, Gran?"

Kayleigh could practically feel Granny's vibrating body over the phone.

"Just go to the website, little girl."

Kayleigh put her phone on speaker and logged onto the website. She scrolled down until she found the page announcing the most recent winning lottery numbers.

"Did you see?" Granny's voice boomed through the phone.

"Let me get the tickets from the other room." Kayleigh set the laptop on the coffee table and dashed into the kitchen. She grabbed the two tickets and returned to the living room.

"Okay, Gran, I'm back." Kayleigh held her breath as she entered the numbers on the website. "Holy moly," she said, exhaling with a whoosh.

"Kayleigh, honey, you won!" Granny shouted. "Check the other one."

Kayleigh sucked in another breath and held it while she entered the numbers from the second ticket. A little over a hundred and fifty thousand dollars.

"Gran, this money is yours."

"No, no, no, sweet girl. I bought those for you. I knew in my spirit you'd win a little something to help you out."

"I can't accept this. You need this more than I do."

"Pshaw, child. Please use this to pursue your dream."

Kayleigh tried to argue, but Granny held firm.

"I'm hanging up now, Kayleigh. No more arguments. You take that money and get yourself a music career."

Kayleigh stared at the blank phone screen after

Granny disconnected. She squealed, startling the dogs. They jumped to their feet and nosed her leg.

She took several yoga breaths before checking the lottery website on how to claim her winnings.

Holden limped upstairs and sank onto the end of his bed, mentally berating himself. Why had he kissed her? Kayleigh had run away like he had the plague. Which he did. Maybe the taste of ice cream wasn't enough to cover the bad taste from his coughing.

But he'd kissed her.

And Kayleigh had kissed him back. Holden's skin tingled where she'd wrapped her arms around him. Even through his T-shirt, he still felt the imprint of her fingers on his ribcage.

What was he supposed to do now? Go on with the knowledge he was in love with the fiery redhead? And he'd never see her again because she was headed for stardom in the country music capital of the world.

He stared at his phone, deciding if he should send Kayleigh a text. What should he say? Sorry, not sorry? Please don't leave?

How pathetic and needy.

Holden stood and pulled the covers back, sank onto the pillow, and pulled the blankets over his head.

JANE DALY

Chapter 35

SIX MONTHS LATER

Holden raised his eyes to meet Jenna's stare.

"What?" he demanded.

"I'm wondering how long you're going to mope around and pine for her."

Holden shifted on the leather theater chair. "I'm not pining."

Andrew slapped him on the back of the head. "You're pining."

Yes, Holden was pining but he'd never admit it to his siblings.

Andrew reached for the remote and stopped the movie. Holden didn't care. He hadn't been paying attention anyway.

Jenna rose from her recliner and stood facing him. "You're an idiot, you know that?"

Holden raised his shoulders and let them drop. Six months and he hadn't heard one word from Kayleigh. No text, no voice mail, heck, not even a smoke signal.

Jenna put her hands on her hips. "Now that your scans came back clear of cancer, you need to stop lallygagging around and go after her."

"I agree," Andrew said. "I'm sick and tired of your sorry face."

Holden's mouth rose in a half-smile. "May I remind you that we look exactly the same?"

"Not even," Jenna said. "You look miserable."

Andrew stood and stretched his arms over his head. He turned left and right, and bent over to touch his toes. "Tell you what, H. I'll call Steve and tell him to prepare for a flight to Nashville."

A wasp nest of nerves swarmed in Holden's stomach. "I don't even know where to find her."

Jenna sent him a sly smile. "I do."

This was news. How had he not known his sister and Kayleigh had been in communication?

"Great!" Andrew exclaimed. "Let's get this party started." He pulled out his phone and tapped on the screen with lightning speed. "Okay. That's done. Steve said he can be ready tomorrow."

Holden gulped. "So soon?" What if he arrived in Nashville and Kayleigh didn't want to see him? They hadn't spoken after he'd impulsively kissed her. Heat rose to his cheeks when he remembered the feel of her lips under his. Had he imagined that she'd responded? Those thoughts kept him turning over and over on his bed every night.

Had it been so awful for Kayleigh that she couldn't bear to be around him for another second? Maybe it was his breath. Surely, she'd been turned off by his sickness.

"I'll make reservations at the Gaylord Opryland Hotel," Jenna said pulling her phone from the holder between their recliners. "For a suite," she added, waggling her eyebrows.

"She's not that kind of woman," Holden said.

"Calm down, H. That's why I'm booking a two bedroom suite."

This was moving way too fast. Holden had a reputation in the real estate world as a quick decision-maker. But this? He'd rather wait and calculate his next move. Maybe send Kayleigh an innocuous text. *'Thinking of you. Hope you're well.'* Something like that to see if she responded.

"I know what you're thinking, H," Andrew said, tapping the side of his head. "You need to get on that jet tomorrow and find her. If you don't, I will."

Holden doubted his brother would make a move on Kayleigh, but jealousy still raised its ugly head. He shot to his feet.

"Fine. Obviously, I can't win with the two of you conspiring against me."

"Don't forget Mom and Dad, too."

Holden rubbed a hand across his forehead. "What?"

Jenna laughed. "They've been in touch with Kayleigh, too."

Holden threw up his hands. "My whole family is against me."

Jenna patted him on the shoulder. "No, H. We're for you. We want you to be happy. And it's obvious you've been miserable for months."

Holden stalked to the stairs and paused on the bottom step. "You know what this means, don't you?"

He didn't wait for his siblings' response. As he ascended the stairs, he heard Andrew tell Jenna, "I haven't been to Nashville in ages. Let's take a trip, shall we?"

Holden groaned. Now his brother and sister would

be witnesses to his epic fail when he told Kayleigh how he felt and Kayleigh rejected him.

"I don't know, Kay," Oliver said. "Your songs are amazing, and your voice is unique. I can't understand why we keep getting rejected."

Kayleigh squirmed on Oliver Young's black leather sofa. Gold records in maple frames decorated the soft gray walls of his office. Oliver had thoughtfully set a box of tissues on the inlaid coffee table. She'd gone through more than a box of tissues over the past six months.

"What should I do?" Kayleigh asked, reaching for a tissue to dab at the tears forming in the corners of her eyes.

Oliver stood from his desk and joined her on the sofa. A little too close for Kayleigh's comfort. She scooted an inch toward the armrest.

"There is one thing I haven't mentioned," Oliver said. "There's a slim possibility that one of your songs might be considered by Megan Moroney."

"Seriously? That's amazing." Hope rose in Kayleigh's chest.

"I heard she's looking for another songwriter. I think your 'Blue Jeans, Porch Swings, and Bare Feet' might be a good fit." He laid a hand on her thigh, just above the knee. "In fact, I have her agent's number. Want me to give him a call?" His grip on her leg tightened.

Kayleigh swallowed. She'd been hit on by pub crawlers and knew how to rebuff them without making them angry. But in the six months she'd been working with Oliver Young, he'd never once made a move.

"Sure. Call him." Kayleigh scooted forward and tried to stand, but Oliver's hand held her down.

"I'll need some incentive."

"Like a monetary incentive?" Kayleigh asked. She'd blown through most of her lottery winnings, but still had a few thousand dollars.

Oliver leaned closer. Kayleigh felt his hot breath on her cheek.

"I was thinking of something a bit more ... personal."

Their faces were inches apart. Kayleigh's thoughts ping-ponged from the last time she'd been this close to a man—Holden—and what this jerk was asking her to do. The question was, how badly did she want to see her songs in the hands of an accomplished professional? Badly enough to actually sleep with this guy? Hard pass.

Kayleigh used her elbow to stab the pointy end into Oliver's rib. She shot to her feet and turned a furious look down on him.

"You're fired. I'm taking my songs and terminating my contract."

Oliver's mouth dropped open. "But—"

"But nothing. We're done."

She gathered her purse and brand-new guitar in its shiny case. "My attorney will be contacting you."

Kayleigh had no attorney, but Oliver didn't know that. She strode from his office in downtown Nashville, located above one of the many bars lining Broadway. Pausing on the sidewalk, she looked up at Oliver's corner window and mentally shook her fist.

There was only one man she would give herself to.

Unfortunately, she'd left him behind in Lake Seneca. She'd been plagued with guilt over leaving Holden the way she did. But she'd needed to see if she could make it in Nashville.

The death of a dream should be more painful, shouldn't it? Part of her felt relieved. Like a closing chapter of a book, Kayleigh was ready to move on.

Samantha had told her about the nonprofit she'd gotten involved with, helping foster girls who were aging out of the system. Sam had begged Kayleigh to bring her guitar and show the girls how to play. Kayleigh had been too busy since she'd left the Donaldson's. Playing in bars and opening with one or two songs for someone further along had kept her busy. She and Oliver had gone from place to place, getting to know 'people' who might be interested.

Kayleigh dashed the tears streaming down her face with the back of one hand.

"Now what?" she said aloud.

Tourists streamed by her, oblivious to her distress. Every head swiveled from right to left, hoping to catch a glimpse of Garth Brooks, Blake Shelton, or Dierks Bentley on the busy streets of Nashville.

Kayleigh moved from the edge of the sidewalk and hunched next to the building. She pulled out her phone to order an Uber to take her back home.

She spied a text from Jenna.

Jenna: Hey, girl. I have a suite at the Gaylord Opryland. Come over and keep me company. I'll send a car. What's your address?

Good old Jenna. They'd become text friends since she'd left Lake Seneca. It was a back door way of keeping track of Holden. She'd been relieved when

Jenna informed her of Holden's good doctor report. Clear scans meant no more cancer. What a relief.

A few days at an exclusive resort hotel was just what Kayleigh needed to recuperate from Oliver's nasty advances. She shuddered, remembering the feel of his hand, hot on her thigh.

Kayleigh tapped out a response with the address of Oliver Young's office.

Jenna: Watch for a white Cadillac Escalade. License plate HH1

Kayleigh smiled. Holden Holdings One. Of course they had a car in Nashville. Why not? Wealthy people had staff.

She'd learned a lot in six months about money management. She was actually good at it. And enjoyed the feeling of setting up a budget and fending off sharks who circled, hoping for a bit of her winnings.

Dad was super proud she'd spent her winnings wisely. Perhaps it was time to talk to Dad about joining his firm. She'd shake the Nashville grime off her feet and head in a new direction.

What about Holden?

That still, small voice was more like a shout in her ears.

"I'll ask Jenna," Kayleigh muttered. "He's probably moved on. As he should." The thought of Holden with some New York City beauty felt like a blow to her chest.

"Ugh. I hate her already." People on the sidewalk widened their circle around her when she spoke out loud.

Before Kayleigh could dwell on her feelings about Holden, a white SUV pulled up and the driver double-tapped on the wheel before springing out and opening the back passenger door.

"Kayleigh McGuire?" he asked.

"That's me."

The driver relived her of the guitar case and stowed it in the back of the vehicle. He closed her door and returned to the driver's seat.

"Let's be on our way," he said.

Chapter 36

Kayleigh stepped out of the SUV and waited for the driver to retrieve her guitar case. He handed it to her with a flourish.

She stepped into the lobby and surveyed her surroundings. She'd been to the Gaylord Opryland Hotel once before for a meeting with her former agent and producer and a music guy from New York.

Kayleigh had been awed then, and she was awed now. Beyond the registration desk was an indoor river with greenery tumbling down the boulders lining the sides of the water feature. The skylight-like roof let in natural night, creating a jungle feel. Guests had their choice of restaurants, but the most popular was the one artfully laid out among the plants and slow-moving river.

Before heading to the desk to inquire about where Jenna was, Kayleigh turned left to head to the ladies room. A familiar voice stopped her.

"Kayleigh? Over here."

She turned to see Andrew lounging against the fence, built to keep guests from dipping their hands or toes into the flowing water.

Andrew strode toward her and pulled her into a hug.

"I didn't know you were here, too," Kayleigh said, lifting her cheek for Andrew's peck.

"Oh, yeah. Jenna and I are having a little brother-sister time."

Kayleigh wanted to ask about Holden, but thought it best to keep silent. She'd pump Jenna for information when they got together.

Andrew hooked his arm through hers. "Let me take you up to our suite."

Kayleigh allowed herself to be led down several halls to an elevator. The elevator had three glass walls. As it rose, Kayleigh swallowed her queasiness. Heights weren't her thing.

The elevator doors swished open to a long hall.

"It's at the end," Andrew said.

Kayleigh's hand grew damp as she clutched the guitar case. Her footsteps dragged as they drew closer to the door to the suite. Jenna would want every detail of her confrontation with Oliver Young, but Kayleigh needed time to sort out her disappointment and revulsion.

Andrew pulled a key card from his pocket and held it over the reader. After the beep and green light, he grasped the handle and pushed open the door.

"After you," he said.

Kayleigh stepped into the suite and was immediately struck with its beauty. A yellow sofa dominated the room, flanked by patterned side chairs in purple and yellow. Somehow it all worked, making the room homey.

"Look who I found wandering around downstairs," Andrew said.

"Kayleigh!" Jenna strode toward her and pulled her

into a hug.

Kayleigh burst into tears. The past couple of hours had finally caught up to her. Oliver's nasty suggestion, more rejection of her music, and the death of her dream of being a country music star.

Jenna rubbed circles on Kayleigh's back. "There, there. It's going to be all right."

A bedroom door crashed open and Kayleigh watched over Jenna's shoulder as Holden stepped into the room with his usual frown.

"What's going on? Who's crying?" He froze, and his mouth dropped open. "Oh."

One of his siblings should have warned him Kayleigh was here. His heart leapt into his throat. Seeing her in person hitched his breath. She was more beautiful than he remembered, even with tears making her eyes red and cheeks blotchy.

"Hi." Holden managed to choke out the one syllable word.

Kayleigh pulled away from Jenna's embrace and used her fingers to wipe her eyes. "Hi."

Holden and Kayleigh locked eyes. He couldn't look away. He wanted to drink in her face, her hair, her body, and everything about her.

He hardly noticed when Andrew and Jenna crept out the door, leaving them alone.

"Hi," he said again. He cursed himself for being unable to speak. Holden took a step toward her. "I missed you."

A deep sigh escaped her lips. "I missed you, too," Kayleigh said. She leaned to one side and set her guitar case on the floor.

She straightened, and Holden took the last few steps into Kayleigh's personal space.

Holden placed his hands on her shoulders and pulled her close.

"Why were you crying?"

Kayleigh's eyes filled with pain. Seeing her cry was torture. She fell into him, her tears wetting his shirt. When she was cried out, Holden led Kayleigh to the sofa and pulled her down next to him.

"What happened?" Holden ran his hand down the length of her hair. It felt exactly as he'd imagined a thousand times over the past six months. Silky and thick, the stands poured through his fingers.

"I'm the dumbest person ever." Kayleigh sniffled and covered her face with her hands.

"Surely not the dumbest." Holden's attempt at humor fell flat.

Kayleigh brought her head up and met his gaze. "Why do I always trust the wrong men?"

Holden felt a flutter of panic. Was she talking about him? Had Kayleigh found out he'd gone behind her back to find Gary Golden, her former producer, manager, or whatever he claimed to be?

While Holden tried to form words, Kayleigh said, "Oliver Young is a pig."

Who was Oliver Young? Holden searched his memory for any previous mention of the man.

Kayleigh's face suffused with color. "Can you believe after six months of paying for studio time, paying for expensive dinners to meet the 'right people,' that he would put me in contact with Megan Moroney's agent? All I had to do was sleep with him."

Who was Megan Moroney? Holden's knowledge of country music could fit into a shot glass. But his pulse spiked thinking of some guy propositioning Kayleigh.

Holden's fists clenched. "I hope you punched him in the face."

Kayleigh sniffed a half-laugh and half-sob. "I elbowed him with everything I've got. Then I told him he was fired, and he'd be hearing from my attorney."

"Atta girl. Who's your attorney?"

Kayleigh looked down to her clasped hands. "I don't have one."

Holden smiled. "I can help with that."

"So, anyway …"

"Anyway? Does that mean you're coming home? To New York?"

Kayleigh nodded. "Yup. I'm done with Nashville. Done with trying to become something I'm not."

Holden put an arm around Kayleigh's shoulders and pulled her to him. "You are an amazing song writer and you have a beautiful voice. You'll find an outlet for your gift."

He felt Kayleigh shudder against his chest as she sobbed again.

Just don't leave again.

Holden pulled in a breath and released it. "I have something to tell you. I found your Golden person. He's currently in jail for fraud."

Kayleigh pulled away. "Really? You did that? For me?"

Holden nodded. "I couldn't bear the thought of him taking advantage of you and stealing your money."

Holden relaxed with Kayleigh's face broke into a broad grin. "Awesome. Let's get Oliver Young, too."

Kayleigh and Holden talked until they were famished. She let him order room service which they devoured. A hamburger in the Gaylord Opryland Hotel tasted better than any backyard barbecue. A girl could get used to this.

Naw. She'd miss the feel of grass tickling her bare feet. But this was pretty darn close.

Holden wiped the last of the grease from the burger and fries from his fingers and tossed his cloth napkin on the tray. Kayleigh's heart quickened when he pinned her with his amazing blue eyes.

Holden cleared his throat. "I have something to say." He glanced around the room before his gaze settled on hers again.

"I know my lifestyle isn't exactly blue jeans and bare feet."

Kayleigh's mouth turned up in a grin. He remembered her song.

"But these past six months have been brutal for me." Holden reached for her hand. Kayleigh let him entwine his fingers with his. "The truth is, I'm not whole without you."

Kayleigh held her breath as Holden seemed to struggle to say more.

"You mean, 'you complete me?'" she said, quoting the famous line from the movie, *Jerry McGuire*.

"Exactly." Holden's shoulders rose and fell. "Do you think you could, you know, be …"

"Yes! A thousand times yes." Kayleigh sent him a grin. "As long as you don't go back to being Mr. Cranky Pants."

"Is that what you called me?"

"Well, not to your face. But behind your back, yes."

Holden stood and pulled her to her feet. "It's a deal."

Kayleigh gazed into his eyes and knew she'd found her purpose. Not to be a country music icon, but to love and be loved by this man.

Did you read Billionaire and the Baker? Get it here.

Sign up for Forget Me Not Romances newsletter and receive a special gift compiled from Forget Me Not Authors!

Join our FB pages to keep up on our most current news!

Winged Publications

JANE DALY

Made in United States
Troutdale, OR
08/02/2025